RUN

L.N. Cronk
Jenn Faulk

Edited by Barbie Halaby

ISBN-13:978-0-9913812-8-9

Rivulet Publishing, West Jefferson, NC

And we know that in all things God works for the good of those who love him, who have been called according to his purpose. Romans 8:28

PENNINGTON SENTENCED TO DEATH

AUSTIN—After a lengthy capital murder trial, Luke Pennington was sentenced to death late Friday by 200th District Court Judge Mark Wise.

Pennington broke down and sobbed as Judge Wise addressed him directly, saying, "You are hereby sentenced, in accordance with Texas law, to death."

On Thursday, Pennington was convicted of two counts of capital murder in the shooting deaths of his 19-year-old former girlfriend, Heather Goodlet, and her roommate, 20-year-old Stacy Kemp. Nearly fifteen months ago, on November 18th, the bodies of Goodlet and Kemp were found in a secluded area of Morgan National Park by police after Pennington flagged down a motorist on nearby Highway 121. The motorist testified that Pennington, who jumped in front of her car and begged her to call police, was covered in blood.

During the trial, Pennington testified on his own behalf. He stated that he had visited with Goodlet and Kemp before deciding to go for a jog by himself on a trail through the woods. Pennington maintains that when he returned from his run he found the girls lying on the ground, already dead.

Investigators determined that both victims were shot in the head with a 9mm handgun and subsequently raped post-mortem. Pennington's DNA and other forensic evidence linked him to the deaths of both women.

Michelle James, a close friend of Goodlet, testified that two days before the murder, Goodlet approached her, crying and saying that she had just broken up with Pennington. According to James, Goodlet stated that they'd had a fight and that "the relationship was over."

Phone records show that Pennington called Goodlet several hours before the murders occurred. Prosecutors theorized that while Pennington somehow convinced Goodlet to meet him at the park, she was obviously concerned for her personal safety and had asked Kemp to accompany her so that she would not be alone when she met with Pennington.

Pennington contended that he and Goodlet had made up earlier that day when he called her and that Goodlet had been the one who suggested meeting at Morgan National Park. Pennington testified that Kemp had joined her because Goodlet had "been having some trouble with her car," and Kemp had offered to drive her.

During his closing statements, defense attorney Paul Baldwin emphasized to jurors that no trace of gunpowder residue was found on Pennington or on any of his clothing. Baldwin also reminded jurors that the murder weapon has never been found.

"If Mr. Pennington had a gun," Baldwin asked the jury, "where did it go? How could a weapon simply disappear?" Baldwin told jurors that the only logical explanation was that the real killer had taken the gun when they fled the scene—before Pennington returned from his jog.

It took the jury less than two days to reach a verdict.

Pennington's formal sentencing took place Friday afternoon after the parents of both victims delivered impact statements to a packed courtroom. "He took my world," said Maya Goodlet, Heather Goodlet's mother. Her voice trembled with emotion as she added, "When he killed her, he killed me, too."

After the sentence was handed down, family and friends of the victims expressed relief.

"I'm just so happy that justice was served today," Alexis Kemp-Randolph, the 23-year-old sister of Stacy Kemp, stated outside the courtroom. "This has changed our family forever—it has changed everything forever."

When asked if she could ever forgive her sister's killer, Kemp-Randolph replied, "Never. What he did to my sister—to both of those sweet, innocent girls—is absolutely unforgivable."

Recent NFL first-round draft pick Trevor Rutledge, who was Kemp's boyfriend at the time she was murdered, agreed. "There's a special place in hell for people like that," Rutledge stated. "When they fry him, I want to be the one to flip the switch."

Pennington's attorney stated that his client would file an appeal to the verdict in addition to the appeals that automatically accompany a death sentence.

Miss Rutledge—

I am very sorry to bother you, but I wrote a letter to your brother a few weeks ago and haven't heard back. I really need to talk to him and I was hoping that you could help me to get in touch with him somehow.

I don't blame Trevor for not answering since he probably thinks that I killed his girlfriend, but I want both of you to know that I did NOT kill Stacy or Heather. I know I was found guilty, but I *promise* you that I didn't do it.

I loved Heather with all of my heart and I cry every time I think about what someone did to her. I miss her so much. Whenever something happens to me, my first thought is that I'm going to tell Heather, but then I remember that I can't. I still can't believe she's gone.

If Trevor thinks that I'm guilty I understand why he hasn't answered me. If I knew who killed Heather I wouldn't want to talk to them either. But I didn't do it and if there is *any* way you could convince him to answer me, I really would appreciate it. I just need to talk to him.

Thank you very much.

Sincerely,
Luke Pennington

Mr. Pennington,

How did you get my name? How did you find my address? And why would you think for one second that I want to do anything to help you?

My brother isn't answering his own mail these days. I'm not sure what kind of contact you have with the outside world there in prison, but in case you haven't heard, Trevor has started his career in the NFL and has moved on with his life. We doubted for a long time that he would be able to, since he was completely and totally devastated when he lost Stacy. But I guess that's no concern of yours since you "Did NOT kill Stacy or Heather."

I don't believe you.

So I'm not going to send your message along to Trevor. I hardly get to talk to him myself, given the schedule he's keeping these days, and the last thing I would ever do is bring this nightmare up again and potentially sabotage the peace he's been able to find.

We've moved on. We've made our peace, all of us. I would suggest, Mr. Pennington, that you do the same. Please don't contact me again.

Audrey Rutledge

Miss Rutledge—

    My lawyer gave me copies of everything that he had from my case and your name and address were in there. I am very sorry to have upset you—that was never my intent. Please forgive me. I won't bother you again.

    Sincerely,
    Luke Pennington

Mr. Pennington,

Seriously?

When I saw your second letter, I knew I should've just thrown it away. I'd already told you to leave me alone, and I should've known that by writing back, you were clearly not respecting my wishes. I don't need this drama in my life right now. Believe me. I really, really don't need this.

I say that, but you know what I did? I opened your letter anyway. Because I wanted to see what lame excuse you had for writing me.

You were at least nice about writing back. Nice, that is, for a convicted rapist and murderer.

That said, I've gone back and looked at both letters. I've thrown them across the room and yelled a little. And I've picked them back up and read them again.

To be honest, I've read them both over and over again.

I want to tell you off. I should tell you off. I'm still creeped out that you went back into your lawyers' papers and found my name. I'm freaking out about the fact that you know my name and my address.

Apart from being creepy, it's actually kind of pathetic, you know? You sat down and wrote a complete stranger, claiming your innocence, even though you're on death row and have no hope of getting out of that sentence.

Why?

See? I shouldn't have opened your letter! Because now I can't think of anything but how angry I am and why you'd go to so much trouble just to get a message to my brother.

Audrey Rutledge

Audrey—

     I want to talk with Trevor because I have been poring over every bit of information I can find, trying to figure out who killed Stacy and Heather, and the only thing that makes sense to me is that Stacy was the original target. I have absolutely no idea, however, who might possibly want to hurt her.

     I met Stacy a few times when I went to visit Heather at UT, but I didn't know her very well at all and I want to know if Trevor has any insight into who might have wanted to hurt her. I realize that he talked to investigators, but right from the very first day, I was considered the prime suspect and so they never really considered anyone else.

     I would be interested in the names of anyone he remembers her talking about who might be able to provide additional information. I believe that whoever did this knew Stacy and knew she was going with Heather to meet me at the park that day. I don't think this was random.

     If Trevor could give me some idea as to who Stacy might have talked to before she and Heather went to the park, it would be very helpful. I called Heather at about ten in the morning, and they met me at the park around three o'clock, so whoever knew that she was going there probably found out before she left around one-thirty.

     Did she usually eat lunch with anyone? Anyone she might have talked to on their hall?

It's also possible that Stacy was followed. If that's the case, maybe she had been having some problems or concerns that she had mentioned to Trevor. That's all I want to know.

Sincerely,
Luke

Luke,

You want to know about Stacy? Why?

In all the time I've spent thinking through the murders and how they changed our lives, I've never once considered that the killer's intended target was Stacy.

Why would I, though? She was a nice girl. A sweet girl. I mean, I didn't spend a lot of time with her because I was in high school and she was off a couple of hours away at college, so it's not like we were best friends or anything. But still. She was just a regular college student, studying hard, having fun, and living her life. Why would someone have wanted to hurt her?

I just took it for granted that you were guilty, like everyone else did. Psycho, rage-filled ex-boyfriend and all, you know. Because that's what you are, after all.

Oh, yeah, I read an article that came out after the verdict, when I was trying to piece together what had happened. My parents were determined to keep me away from the trial. Too gory, too graphic, too disturbing for a high school kid. But they couldn't keep me from reading what had been determined. And unless I missed some huge piece of evidence that your attorney tried to use as the jury decided your fate, there's no possible way that you could be innocent. You were the only one there. You had their blood all over you. You'd been fighting with Heather.

How gullible do you honestly think I am?

Gullible, says the girl who keeps writing to a convict on death row. And this, Luke, this is the main reason why I'm not going to bother Trevor with all of these requests you've made. I think it'll make him angry enough if he knows that you're trying to pin all of this on Stacy and something she did or someone she offended. But hearing that his little sister is now unofficial pen pals with her killer? I think that just might be too much for him.

So, no. I won't ask Trevor any questions. And it's not like he would have had answers. Do you think he and Stacy were connected at the hip? How would he have known who Stacy and Heather were having lunch with that day? He was off at a football game. Do you think he was texting her from the sidelines, asking where she had gone to lunch? His mind was in other places. They were heading toward the national championship! Well, they *were*, before they had to put in the backup quarterback for those last few games of the season. And why did they have to do that? Because my brother was a wreck and couldn't even think about football. So not only did you take Stacy from him, but you took that championship from him as well. From Stacy, too, because she was his biggest fan. She never missed a game. She always made those away games an excuse for a road trip. She probably struggled in half her classes because of all the early weekends she took so that she could drive out to Trevor's games—

Except . . . she didn't go out of town that weekend. She stayed home.

Oh, wow.

She didn't go to watch Trevor play that weekend. And if she was in the park that afternoon, where you killed her, it means that she wasn't even watching it on television. That wasn't like her at all! Or at least not what I knew of her . . .

There's something not right about all of this. Do you think she and Trevor . . .

Did Heather say anything to you about what was going on with my brother and Stacy? Were they having problems?

Oh, good grief. Why am I still writing you this?

I'm done. I don't know anything, Luke. I'm not getting in touch with Trevor.

I'm not going to keep on talking to you about this. You've given me no real concrete reason to think that the jury was wrong when they convicted you. And beyond that, my brother will kill me if he finds out that we've been writing to each other.

Seriously. Leave me alone.

Audrey

Audrey—

I have lots of concrete evidence, but how old are you? You're in high school?? Most of the evidence I have is stuff that a high school kid doesn't really need to be hearing about. That's why I need to talk to Trevor.

I don't have any idea if Stacy and Trevor were having problems. Stacy didn't say anything about it at all and she used his car to drive Heather to the park, so I'm kind of thinking that things were okay between the two of them. Heather and I went for a walk alone, and Stacy stayed in the car to study because she said she had a test on Monday. Heather said that she had been quizzing her for it during the entire drive. That's probably the only reason Stacy didn't go to the game.

In my appeal, I'm going to have an affidavit from Stacy's chemistry professor stating that she really did have a test coming up and I'm going to make sure they know that her textbook and notebook were in the car. My lawyer didn't bring up any of that, and I think he should have. When I appeal, I'm going to make sure a lot of stuff is included. I kept asking my lawyer about why he wasn't bringing certain things up, but he kept blowing me off and telling me that he had things taken care of . . . and I believed him.

Talk about gullible.

Even though he didn't bring up stuff that I thought he should have, I never for one second thought I was going to be convicted. I couldn't believe it when they said I was guilty, but now I know that I should have done a better job of making sure that everything that didn't make sense was shown to the jury during the trial. It's

18

too late to do anything about that now, but I do realize that I've got to do everything within my power to make sure the same kind of mistakes don't happen during my appeal.

That's what made me go back over the evidence so carefully, and going back over the evidence so carefully is what made me really start to think that someone was after Stacy . . . that this wasn't just something random. I think someone was after her and that Heather was just in the wrong place at the wrong time. She got in the way, and that's why both of them are dead now.

I don't want you to get in trouble with your brother, but you don't have to tell him that you wrote to me. Maybe you could just tell him that I wrote to you and see if he mentions that I wrote to him, too? Could you maybe just see if he even got my letter?

If not, I understand, and I'm sorry to bother you. Thank you for taking the time to write me back.

Sincerely,
Luke

Luke,

You have lots of concrete evidence, huh? I'm sure the only reason you don't want to share it with me is because you think I'm too young. I think the real reason you don't want to get into concrete evidence, though, is because you know that all of it points straight to you.

Like the undisputed fact that your semen was discovered inside of Heather. I may be young and gullible, but I'm pretty sure you had something to do with that. That alone seems like enough evidence to condemn you, and apparently, what the jury heard just further solidified that conclusion.

I'm not sure what you're hoping to accomplish with these letters. I hear what you're saying about Stacy and all that your lawyer didn't bring up. But what difference would any of that make? The presence of those things doesn't point to your innocence. Are there other things that your lawyer left out that are better than this? Is there any real reason—any solid, glaring reason—that you think someone was after Stacy? Did it have anything to do with my brother?

Because if it didn't, I don't know what any of this has to do with me.

If you're guilty, I hope you find peace before you die. And if you're not guilty . . . well, I hope you find a whole lot of more compelling evidence. But of course, you are guilty.

Goodbye, Luke.

(Oh, and I'm not in high school. I'm 19 and a sophomore in college. The same age that Heather was when you killed her, and old enough to know when someone is lying to me.)

Audrey

Dear Audrey—

A sophomore in college, huh? Well, then, at 19 you should be old enough to know that there are other ways for semen to get inside of a woman besides rape.

After Heather and Stacy got there, Heather and I went for a walk so we could be alone and while we were gone, we made love. I told the police about that as soon as they questioned me.

I have never backtracked or changed anything that I said to them because I have been telling the truth all along and all of the evidence supports what I say happened. For some reason, though, nobody else will even consider that I'm telling the truth.

I took investigators to the exact spot where Heather and I made love. Would I have done that if it was a place I had raped her? I could have said that I didn't remember where it had happened and hoped they never found it. I cooperated with them completely because I didn't have anything to hide and because I wanted to do whatever I could to help them find the killer. But instead of agreeing that it supported my story, they wrote down that it looked like there "had been a struggle." They pinned me for it right from the beginning and never considered anybody else.

Heather had no injuries or defensive wounds of any kind. If I had raped her, wouldn't she have fought back? Wouldn't I have had some scratches or marks on me? The forensic evidence showed that Heather got dressed and walked around after we made love. This also corroborates what I told investigators, which is that afterward, we got dressed and walked back to the parking area where Stacy was waiting.

The autopsy results said that both of them were raped *after* they were killed. How do you explain that if I'm not telling the truth? What do you think happened? That I raped her, let her get dressed and walk back to the car, and then killed her and raped her again? If this is really what happened, then why didn't Stacy do something to help Heather the first time she was being raped? Or why didn't she at least run and get help?

Both girls were raped with some kind of blunt object. Why? Why kill two girls and then rape them with some kind of object after they were dead? There was no sign of a struggle at all. Someone just walked up to them, shot them dead, and then tried to make it look like they were raped. What kind of motive would someone possibly have for doing something like that? I think someone was trying to divert attention from what was really going on by making it look like it was rape.

Can you honestly tell me that what I'm saying doesn't make sense?

Luke

Luke,

You're never going to stop writing me, are you? Most girls my age have normal lives. You know, classes, nights out with friends, going out on dates. Me? I've got my mailbox and my trusty correspondence with a man on death row.

Fun times.

That said, I read your letter. And wow, you're right. So much of what you said makes absolutely no sense . . . especially when held up next to what the jury already decided.

Let's start with this.

Heather's friend testified that Heather had broken up with you and that your relationship was over. Completely over. Yet she met up with you. Your story and the real story match up on that point. But you're trying to tell me that she met up with you, a man she was done with, then wandered off and randomly had sex with you. In the woods.

Who does that, Luke? Really, do people do things like that? Because it all sounds a little dramatic. A little too dramatic. Made up, in other words.

Then you're trying to tell me that the semen wasn't connected to the post-mortem rape. Which fits your story, of course, but how can the forensic evidence be so certain? If they could pinpoint that there were two different encounters—one where you had consensual sex and another where you raped her—then why wasn't that compelling enough evidence to bring into the trial?

And raped with a blunt object? What are you talking about? Why? Is this real evidence, or are you just making things up now?

I'm seriously angry with my parents right now for not letting me be there at the trial because I don't know what to believe. I'll admit that some of what you're saying makes sense and really makes me wonder if you're telling the truth, but I only have your word. Nothing else. You could be lying to me. You probably are lying to me. Why should I believe you? And if there was such "obvious" evidence of your innocence, why were you the only suspect? Do the police have something against you? Isn't it more likely they know a whole lot that you're not telling me?

Why should I believe you? I shouldn't, right?

Let's just say I did. Why not? Just me and my convict pen pal, playing the what if game. If I was to believe you, there are still some things that don't make any sense.

Like this. If Heather wasn't afraid of you (and I certainly believe that she was, because all the evidence points to that), then why did she bring Stacy with her? And if the two of you were on the outs and she'd broken up with you and she'd brought Stacy with her for moral support or whatever, what kind of friend was Stacy to let her go off with you into the woods? Furthermore, if Stacy was on the outs with someone or being harassed herself, like you want me to believe, why would she have hung around alone in a deserted park?

I keep going back to the secluded part of this all, Luke, because it's shady. If you just wanted to meet up with Heather to talk things through (and not to, oh I don't know, kill her and her friend), then why didn't you look up the local Starbucks or something? Why a park? Why take her off into the woods?

Or, honestly, why didn't you just meet her back at school? Did you go to school with her? Where did you meet her? What kind of relationship did you have? Why had she broken up with you? Why were you so insistent on seeing her again?

This whole thing is shady. Did the police ever believe that you were able to convince her to go off with you, or do they think that you just showed up and killed both girls immediately?

Either you're the worst criminal ever, given how blatant the evidence is against you, or you are the unluckiest man in the world to have wandered into this situation. I mean, you look so guilty.

If what you're saying is true, then why didn't you—after you made love to the woman you professed to love—send Stacy on and take Heather home yourself? How could you have reconciled with her, been intimate with her, then gone off for a run, expecting that she'd just wait there for you to get back? What kind of man does that? After all that you said about how much you loved her and how you still miss her, how did you just leave her after being with her like that? Maybe I'm a hopeless romantic (and you're just a hardened criminal, so I see how you wouldn't be able to understand that), but surely there would have been some tenderness after that. Wanting to take her home. Wanting to take care of her. Wanting to celebrate what had just been restored. Not, "Hey, baby, wait for me while I go on a run."

Who does that? And what kind of girl (and her friend, who probably didn't like you much after all the drama you'd put Heather through) would have been fine with that?

That, Luke. That just doesn't make any sense. Apart from the romantic notions I naively have that bring the validity of all of that into question, it just doesn't make sense on a practical level. Why would they have waited there for you? They had my brother's car. They could have left. By your admission, you and Heather were fine with each other. Mission accomplished.

Why didn't she and Stacy just go back home?

Audrey

Audrey—

I'm never going to stop writing you? You're the one who won't stop writing me! The only reason I wrote back to you in the first place is because you asked me a question. I told you I wouldn't bother you anymore, and then you wrote me again and asked me another question. If you don't want me to write to you, then why do you keep asking questions? Maybe it's because deep down what you really want is the truth. Your most recent letter had so many questions in it that it's going to take me three hours to answer them all. Good thing I've got plenty of time on my hands.

First of all, random sex? What was random about it? We had a fight. We made up. We were glad to see each other again and we were glad we were back together. It wasn't random. And we didn't "wander off in the woods." We went away from the car and away from Stacy because we wanted to be alone. What's so hard to understand about that?

Also, she wasn't done with me. WE MADE UP! How many times do I have to say that? If she hadn't been killed, no one would blink twice at the thought that a couple could break up and then actually get back together, but since she got killed, apparently it's impossible.

Yes, they determined absolutely that Heather and I'd had sex *before* she was killed and that she had been raped with a blunt object *after* she died. I don't know how to explain this to you without being graphic, but there was semen on her underwear. The only way for this to happen is if we made love and then she got redressed again and walked around. You know, gravity? But when I found her and Stacy, both of them were naked from the waist down and they had definitely been raped after they were shot. Whoever did it used a stick or something and injured them internally. Their injuries were severe—so severe that if they had been alive when it happened, there would have been a lot more blood. But since their hearts weren't beating when it happened, the bleeding was "consistent with post-mortem injuries." That was about the only thing throughout this whole ordeal that has brought me any peace—the knowledge that Heather wasn't alive when she was raped.

I already told them in court why Heather didn't come alone. The check engine light was on in her car and she didn't know why. It turns out that she was just due for an oil change, but she didn't know that at the time and she was worried about it. She told Stacy and Stacy offered to drive her. It wasn't for moral support and I never said that Stacy was on the outs with someone or being harassed. I just said that I thought she was the original target. I have no idea if she knew anything about it. That's why I want to talk with Trevor.

You say that you keep going back to the secluded part of it and that it's shady. Well, you know what? If I'd known then what I know now, I definitely would have suggested a Starbucks or something, but I had no reason to believe that we couldn't meet safely in a park. Both of us had a lot to do, but when we decided that we really wanted to see each other, I did offer to go to her. She said she didn't want to make me do that so we talked about getting together somewhere halfway instead. Heather knew that I was going to miss cross-country practice and she's the one who suggested meeting at the park so that I could still get my run in. They have good trails there, but like I said, if I'd known, I never would have agreed to it.

You asked me a lot of questions about my relationship with Heather. I've known her since junior high and we started dating when she was a junior and I was a senior. She asked me to prom and we've been together ever since. She was the most important person in my life.

It's none of your business why we broke up.

I wanted to see her again because we made up and I loved her. How can you not understand that I wanted to see her again and that she wanted to see me? Obviously you've never been in love before. I would do anything if I could see her again right now. Sorry if you don't get that.

I did not want to leave Heather after we made love, but I had to get my run in. I ran track for Solberg University—the 800 and the mile. Those are mid-distance events, but the coach made us run cross-country in the fall to stay in shape. We were going to say goodbye, but neither one of us really wanted to. I only had to run about five miles so we decided that I'd go ahead and do that before it got dark and then maybe the three of us would go grab some dinner in Cedarton. Stacy was fine with that because she was still studying away. Heather offered to quiz her some more while I was gone. When I left, they were heading over to the picnic table with Stacy's textbook and notes.

You got any more questions or am I done hearing from you? I bet I know the answer to that. For what it's worth, Heather was a hopeless romantic, too.

Luke

Luke,

You just LIED to me!

You've already told me that Stacy's textbook and notebook were in my brother's car. And then, in your last letter, you said that she and Heather were heading over to the picnic table at the park WITH the textbook and the notes when you left.

So, which is it? The textbook and the notes were with the girls or in the car?

I know that seems like a silly point to linger on because it's just a textbook, right? What does it matter? It could matter a whole lot if you saw it in one place and it was in another when you came back.

Or was it?

I think you're telling so many lies that you're confusing yourself, Luke. It's hard to keep track of what you said when you're making it all up, huh?

And while I appreciate your tragic love story angle, I find it very, very interesting that you're being vague about why you and Heather were having problems.

Well, maybe not vague. No, saying, "It's none of your business" is just being rude.

Guess what, buddy? You made ALL of this my business when you tracked me down like some stalker, wrote me a creepy letter telling me about how much you loved a girl you've been convicted of murdering, and kept trying to get me to talk to my brother about it all.

And I am not a hopeless romantic. Even if I were, nothing about your story is romantic. And, no, FYI, I've never been in love, and if you're a clear representation of what most men are like, writing such rude and angry letters screaming in ALL CAPS like you did at me, the only person in the whole world who's willing to hear you out . . .

Well. I don't know that I want to fall in love if most men are like you.

There you go, Luke. You've turned me off to all men. Well done, sir. Well done.

Am I right, though? Am I the only person in the entire world who's willing to hear you out? Because I get the sense that no one (me included) believes you, so you think you'd jump on the chance to tell your side of the story to someone, anyone, instead of belittling and picking on the one person who OPENS EVERY LAST ONE OF YOUR LETTERS!

See? I can get angry in all caps, too. How did that feel, Luke? Want me to yell at you about how you just don't understand life like I do, just like you yelled at me? It must be a terrible burden to be as wise as you are when it comes to love and loss. Pity the rest of us idiots, who will never know such profound love like you did. Must make you feel like an even bigger martyr, suffering as you are now, like some tragic hero whose only crime was loving too much.

Give me a break.

I think I need to stop reading your letters because I just get angrier and angrier every time. And I definitely need to stop writing you because even though I ask legitimate questions, you don't give compelling enough answers to convince me that you're innocent. Why was all the evidence you claim to have never used in your trial? Why did the police have you picked as the culprit from the very beginning? Why was the case solved so quickly?

These are legitimate questions, Luke. Questions that just might spell freedom for you if you'll take the time to really answer them instead of insulting and belittling me when I ask them.

Whatever. I'm so done with this.

Oh, and not that it matters, but we have something in common. I'm a runner, too. So I know a few things. And five miles, if you're running competitively at the collegiate level, would have only taken you about half an hour.

In other words, it would have been impossible for you to have left Stacy and Heather studying at a picnic table (with that pesky textbook) only to return half an hour later to find them dead without having seen or heard anything suspicious. If you were having sex at the park, then I'm betting that it was secluded. Any traffic in or out would have been noticed, right? Apart from that, why didn't you hear a gunshot? Five miles means you likely ran two and a half out, then two and a half back. That's not far enough to miss the sound of two gunshots, even at the farthest distance you would have been.

And before you try to give me some lame excuse about how you had earbuds in and that's why you didn't hear anything, I know you weren't listening to music because you ran to get help instead of using your phone to call the police. Why didn't you use your phone? Because you didn't have a phone with you. It was just you and the park around you on that run. You should have heard something, Luke. And on a run that short, you would have surely seen something out of place or not quite right.

So, since you've so kindly asked me to keep on asking you questions, I'll conclude my letter with this.

What did you hear while you were on your run? What was the deal with Stacy's textbook and notes?

And why did Heather break up with you?

Audrey

Dear Audrey—

You are the only person who has written to me since my conviction, so yeah, you're right. No one else is even listening. I was upset, but I shouldn't have been rude to the one person who is willing to correspond with me and ask legitimate questions. I'm very sorry and it won't happen again.

I don't have any idea why Stacy's books were in her car when I got back. Maybe the girls got cold sitting at the picnic table and went back to the car? Maybe the wind kept blowing their papers too much? I really don't know. All I know is that the girls were headed toward the picnic table with Stacy's stuff when I left, and the crime scene photos show that her books were in the car when I got back.

You're right about how long I was gone. Specifically, I was gone exactly 33 minutes and 26 seconds. The last thing I did before I discovered Heather and Stacy was stop my watch and take note of the time. I wish I'd been wearing my GPS watch because that would have corroborated my story, but it wasn't charged and I couldn't find the charger when I was getting ready to leave my apartment, so I just grabbed my regular watch.

Have you ever been to Morgan National Park before? The path I was on is called McRae's Trail. If you don't know where I'm talking about, you can download a park map from their website and look at it. It leads from the parking lot and picnic area where our cars were parked and ends at a small waterfall about 3.2 miles away. It isn't a loop—it just ends at the waterfall. I didn't run all the way to the end because I only needed to go 5 miles total and I was anxious to get back to Heather, so I just ran for exactly 17 minutes and then turned around and went back, confident that I'd gone at least 2.5 miles at that point. Anyway, if you are familiar with McRae's Trail or if you look at a map, you'll see that it runs along the creek the entire way. It's a decent-sized creek, and a lot of the time, it's fairly loud. I never heard any gunshots.

If I was lying, why wouldn't I have just said that I heard them? How would it have benefited me to say that I didn't hear them? I said I didn't hear them because I didn't.

I didn't use my phone to call for help because it was locked in my car and I didn't have my keys. I had given them to Heather when I went for my run. Her pants were near her on the ground and I looked in the pockets for my keys so that I could drive for help, but I couldn't find them. The police later discovered them in the underbrush nearby. I have no idea how they got there. Anyway, I looked for them as much as I could and tried to get into both of the cars but they were locked. That's why my bloody fingerprints were found on the door handle of Trevor's car—I wanted to look and see if my keys were in there.

The stupid thing is that I never looked for Stacy's keys. It turns out they were in her coat pocket. I could have driven her car for help just as easily as I could have driven mine, but I didn't think about that until I was almost all the way to the road, so I just kept going. When I found the girls I obviously wasn't thinking too clearly. I was scared to death. I remember that when I picked up Heather's jeans to look for my keys, I could hardly even hold them because my hands were shaking so bad.

38

I think I've answered all of your questions, so now let me politely ask you one. What did I shoot the girls with? The gun that was used to kill them was never found. I had no powder residue anywhere on my body. How could that possibly be if I shot them? And where did the gun go? Investigators searched the entire area thoroughly and never found it, so where did it go? And before you suggest that I ran two or three miles in a different direction and threw it over a cliff or something, you should know that the timeline I gave police matches exactly. They determined that both girls died during the time I said I was out for my run. The amount of time it would have taken me to run to the highway and flag somebody down matches too. I didn't have any time to hide the gun somewhere where it couldn't be found.

Thank you for listening.

Luke

Luke,

Evidence, Luke. Evidence.

There was no evidence that you had or fired a gun. I get
that. But what if you'd been wearing gloves and more
clothing that you threw off after the murder? And there's
a creek in that park. A waterfall, even! If the water was
moving fast enough, you could have thrown the gun,
along with anything you were wearing that had
gunpowder residue on it, down there into the water, and
it would've been miles away by the time the police showed
up.

The fact that there isn't evidence may be a big piece of
evidence. The absence of these things, especially at the
park where there was an obvious place for it to all be
thrown and discarded, suggests that whoever did this
had a plan, worked quickly, and threw out everything
that was incriminating.

If you were that "whoever" (and I believe you were, as did
the jury), you flubbed up there toward the end. You
should've gotten out of there. Or maybe hanging around

with a bloody shirt and all of these rumors floating around about your bad relationship with your girlfriend was part of your plan.

Bad plan, Luke.

And you left your GPS watch at home. I'm guessing you use that watch fairly religiously as you're recording your mileage, so how bizarre was it that you would leave it this one time, the one time that it would actually have saved you?

It sure does bring up some questions.

That said, though, you know what confuses me most about all of this? You say you're innocent. You say that there was plenty of evidence that should have cleared you.

But the police never looked at anyone but you. You were their only suspect.

What do they know that I don't know? What led them to be so certain that you were the killer, even if all this evidence you claim exists was present? Why were they so quick to arrest you and press charges?

I'd really like to know what the truth is in all of this. All that I'm seeing points to you, despite what you keep claiming.

So what am I missing?

And seriously, Luke. What was going on with you and Heather?

Because I have a feeling that the answer to that question, about why she broke up with you in the first place, will solve a lot of the mystery.

Audrey

Audrey—

      I can't tell you why Heather and I broke up, but it doesn't have anything to do with what happened, I promise.

      The creek was nowhere fast enough to carry a gun away! Drive out there and look at it and you'll see. Clothing, maybe, but even then you'd think something would have gotten caught in a branch or something and been found, wouldn't you? They went over the entire area with a fine-toothed comb and they found nothing. What makes the most sense is that whoever shot them got in their car and drove away, taking the gun and their gunpowder residue with them. A gun cannot just disappear!

      Did you know that they offered to let me take a plea bargain? They offered me life in prison with no chance for parole, but I said "No," because I was so sure they were going to find me innocent. I was so sure of that because I knew that I was innocent and I knew that there was no way they could prove that I was guilty if I wasn't. If I had to do it all over again, though, I think I would do the same thing. I'm not going to admit that I did something I didn't do. I guess I'd rather die telling the truth.

      I will admit that there's something I can't explain . . . something that is probably why I'm sitting here in a six-by-ten cell. What the police knew that you apparently don't, and why they didn't really look at anybody besides me, is that there was forensic evidence in and on the girls that they linked to me. Dirt and plant matter that was consistent with the parking lot where I keep my car at school. And hair and more DNA. Not semen, but saliva. I can't explain any of that. I'm trying to be honest with you here by telling you about this, but you have to believe me. I don't know how it got there. I don't know what happened. All I know is that I didn't do it. I didn't do it. I did *not* do it.

Luke

Luke,

What?! They found your saliva IN the girls?! Correct me if I'm wrong, Luke, but that's something that can't be faked! Your DNA in the dead bodies! No wonder they found you guilty so quickly!

That's sick. You're sick. This whole thing is sick.

And you still won't answer my question! You still won't tell me what was going on with you and Heather. But I think I know now. I think she knew that you were a sick, demented pervert and deviant. No wonder she broke up with you! No wonder she was so upset! No wonder she was done with you!

Guess what, Luke? So am I.

Done.

Audrey

Audrey—

Deep down I was hoping that you were going to believe me, but I wasn't surprised when I read your letter yesterday.

The chaplain visited with me after I got it. I was pretty upset. I always have a lot of questions for him because so much stuff doesn't make sense to me and he's always really nice about answering my questions and trying to explain things to me. He usually does a pretty good job, but yesterday I just wanted to die and I think he knew that there wasn't anything he was going to be able say to explain to me why this is happening.

He looked at me for a minute and then he finally said, "You know, Luke. No matter who you are, no matter how much education you have, no matter how much you study the Bible, one day you're going to reach a point where there's something that you can't understand. That's when you have to make a decision. Are you going to have faith and believe or not?"

I know he was talking about believing in God, but all of a sudden I realized that's what happened to you. You got to the point where you couldn't understand and you had to make a decision whether you were going to have faith and believe or not.

You chose not, and I can't honestly say that I blame you. Thank you for listening to me as long as you did. It gave me hope for a little while, and I really appreciate it. I promise I won't bother you again.

Luke

Luke,

I got your last letter—two weeks ago, actually. I should've just tossed it straight into the garbage, just like I should've done with your very first letter.

But I didn't. I held onto it.

I wasn't going to read it, of course, because I was done with you and done with this whole mess. But I just couldn't throw it away. I couldn't make myself do it!

So I tried to forget it. As I tried to just be done with it all, my mind kept going back to everything you'd shared, to all the details of the murders, and to your insistence, again and again, that you were innocent. I can't say that I believe you, but at this point, I'm not sure if it matters whether or not I do, because what's most important is what I do know, with absolute certainty.

We're all rotten people, when you get right down to it. And while your particular degree of rotten seems more heinous than mine, I know it's an even playing field in the sight of God. One strike for us both. We're out. Totally out.

Well, I'm not. Not anymore. I didn't tell you this earlier because I didn't think it made any difference to what you were claiming, but I'll say it now, not because it'll help you solve this mystery you act like you have to solve but because I think it might help your heart. When Stacy was killed, it was hard on all of us. My brother was a mess, like I already told you, which means that my parents were completely preoccupied with his grief and their own. In the meantime, they didn't see what it did to me.

I didn't know Stacy all that well, so it wasn't grief that I was feeling exactly. It was more like fear, or dread, knowing life was that fragile, that one moment a young woman with her whole life ahead of her could be discovering what was waiting on the other side of death.

I was scared to even think about it. I mean, I believed in God and thought that being a good person was enough to get me into Heaven or whatever was out there, but I sure didn't know the particulars. Not knowing all the details made me anxious, and in all the questions and fears I had, I decided to get some answers.

So I became a bona fide Bible scholar. Well, kind of. I just started reading, not knowing if things would be any clearer, but after only a few weeks of reading, I discovered some things.

Being good isn't enough. Being the best person I can be isn't enough to win points with God. Unfortunate? Maybe if I was a good person, but as the Bible was quick to tell me, I wasn't good at all! None of us are. I read that I was dead in my sin. What sins, right? Every wrong thought, every unkind word—all sin! I wasn't deserving of anything beyond this life.

But then, the Bible went on to tell me that even though I was no better than a dead dog, God had, in His mercy and His love toward me, paid for all those sins by becoming a man. Fully God, fully man, Jesus Himself, coming to live a perfect life, die a perfect death, and have a perfect resurrection, taking the punishment for my sins and winning eternal life for me.

It made sense. Well, actually, it didn't make sense, because I didn't deserve anything.

That's the thing about God, though. He gives mercy even when we don't deserve it.

Anyway, my life changed from that point on. I believed. I had faith. I was going to live for Him. And I've been doing just that.

And then I got your first letter, and it was like all grace and compassion and mercy left me. I was sure you didn't deserve to even be listened to, honestly, because of what you'd done. Then I felt like you were lying to me, trying to get me to believe your crazy story, and it only made me think you more unworthy. (Unworthy like all of us are, but I was too proud to admit it, you know.)

I was done with you, just like I said.

But your last letter sat there, unopened. And maybe it was hope, hope that I was wrong and that maybe you somehow really were innocent, that made me finally open it.

You said you just wanted to die.

No matter what you've done or what you didn't do, no matter whether you're guilty or innocent, no matter whether or not anyone ever believes you, there's still hope, Luke. There's always hope.

I've been a poor witness to that, and reading that you just want to die? That alone convicted me. But when you went on to say that you were talking to a chaplain, that these are things you're grappling with, and that you know you have to have faith somewhere along the line . . . it's like God had a huge megaphone held up to my ear, yelling, "Heelllllooooo!!!"

I don't know that I believe you when it comes to the murders and whether or not you're innocent. I don't know that I'll ever believe you.

But I do know that my faith doesn't have to be placed in you on this one. I'm putting my faith in God, in watching Him bring the truth to light, and in doing my part to show you that there's reason for hope, even now.

So, please, keep writing me. I want to help you. If you need someone to listen, I want to be there for you. It's less about your guilt or innocence now and more about just showing you hope.

I'm so sorry for what you're going through, Luke. Even if you're guilty, there's no sin so great that it should leave you as hopeless as you sounded in your last letter.

There's always hope.

Audrey

Audrey—

I don't even know where to start. First of all, thank you for your letter. Thank you for compassion. Thank you for saying "even *if* you're guilty" instead of "even though you're guilty." You may not realize that you said that, but you did. I think that deep down you want to believe that I'm innocent.

I really appreciate your offer that I can keep writing to you and I really want you to keep writing me, but I think I need to set the record straight about a few things. I don't want you to think that I've been lying to you or misleading you, so I want to make sure that you're clear on a couple of things—even if it means that I might not hear from you again.

First, apparently I said I wanted to die in my last letter? I don't remember exactly what I said, but I didn't mean I was going to kill myself or anything. I just meant that I was really upset and unhappy. I was miserable. And actually I stayed pretty miserable until I got your letter today, but I wasn't suicidal. I just want to make sure you understand that.

Second, I got the distinct impression that you are assuming my soul is in jeopardy and that you want us to keep writing so that you can make sure I'm saved or whatever. I never said that I didn't believe. I think it's great that you want to show me hope and I really appreciate that and everything, but my faith is actually stronger right now than it's ever been.

So even though you aren't going to have the chance to save my life or my soul, would you still be willing to show me compassion and keep writing? As brothers and sisters in Christ, we're supposed to encourage one another, right? It really is terrible here. I can use all the encouragement I can get.

Sincerely,
Luke

Luke,

Did I say "if" you're guilty? I guess I did. I'm not sure what I believe anymore, as far as the murders go and what happened that day.

Apart from that, my intent in writing you wasn't to "save your soul." How would you react though, as someone of faith, if you got a letter from someone saying that they just wanted to die, which is what you said. Wouldn't you offer what hope you could? I wasn't trying to be pushy or presumptuous. I was just worried about you.

Which sounds really stupid, since I don't really know you. And since I'm still fairly certain that you're a murderer.

Well . . . sort of certain.

It's terrible there, huh? I can't imagine. All I know about prison is what I see on TV shows and movies, and I'm sure that's not entirely accurate. And with you on death row, it must be much worse. It must be awful.

54

Wow. Well, you asked for encouragement, and I'm apparently inept at offering any.

Maybe you should tell me about your life before this. Would that help? Talking about what life was like before all of this happened? About the things you enjoyed, how you spent your days, what kind of dreams you had for the future . . .

Unless that's too depressing.

Help me out here, Luke. Tell me about who you were, who you are.

Audrey

Audrey—

You said, "Sort of certain." That actually made me smile.

Yes, it's terrible here. I saw prison on TV, too, but trust me, this ain't the same thing by a long shot. I am all by myself, completely alone, in a six-by-ten cell. We can't talk to other inmates. On the plus side, I'm not getting beat up or raped, but on the negative side, I have never been so lonely in my entire life. My mother comes to visit me once a month and she cries the whole time she's here. She keeps asking me what she did wrong. My brother writes me less than you do and his letters are full of details about what he and his wife have been doing lately and what he had to eat the last time they went out. He tells me to keep my chin up and things like that. He thinks I'm guilty, too.

Who was I?

I was an athletic science major—I wanted to be an athletic trainer when I graduated. I had a full track scholarship. I used to be in good shape, but I've gained thirteen pounds since I've been in here.

One of the classes I had to take for my major was organic chemistry, and I was in over my head right from the start. We had a four-hour lab every Tuesday afternoon and the only reason I was passing was because of the teaching assistant, Macie.

Macie was a grad student and she always helped me whenever I couldn't figure out what to put down on my lab reports (which was most of the time).

It didn't take Macie long to figure out that I was having just as much trouble in the class as I was in the lab, so she offered to help me. She worked for the professor who taught the class. She said she could get me copies of the tests beforehand. She had access to his computer and to his files. He trusted her.

Thirty bucks a test. I was desperate. I jumped on it—didn't even have to think twice.

That's who I was.

Luke

Luke,

Well, wasn't that a happy little story? As bad as o-chem likely was, there's still that thing called integrity, which is something that should have mattered to you, as an athlete and competitor. I ran a 10K a few weeks back in a rural town, just for training purposes. They didn't even give us chips or have timing mats out—that's how low key this event was. At one point in the course, there weren't any volunteers around, and all the other runners cut a big corner, shaving off a quarter of a mile and cutting down their unofficial time. But do you know what I did, Luke? I ran the entire 6.2 miles. I came in dead last, of course, but I didn't figure finishing first would matter if I didn't actually do the work and run all the miles. It would have been a hollow victory, kind of like those A's you were making in your class.

Why am I lecturing you, though? You said that's who you were. Who are you now? Maybe you've got a new way of looking at justice now that you're paying for a crime that you claim you didn't commit.

There's some irony for you. You got away with something you did do, and now you're paying for something you didn't do.

Or something you say you didn't do.

Keep on smiling if you want to, but I still don't believe you. Not entirely.

Speaking of that, though, and your way of life before all of this happened, it made me think of something. You're convinced that Stacy had someone after her, which may very well be.

But what if the killer was after you? The way you described yourself leaves a lot to be desired in the character department, so maybe you'd so infuriated someone that they were looking for a chance to get back at you. You played right into his hands (or her hands, to be fair) and did a whole lot of really stupid things at the crime scene, of course, but everything that helped to convict you, like Heather telling everyone that you'd broken up and how she was done with you, could have easily compelled the killer to come up with a plan and execute it. You had a clear motive. Maybe someone had something against you, saw their opportunity to ruin your life, and took it.

Maybe Macie was afraid that you were going to turn her in.

No, that seems unlikely. Unless she was certifiably crazy, killing two girls to ensure that you wouldn't turn her in for cheating is a little extreme, right?

Was Heather connected to someone who hated you? You keep avoiding my question about why she broke up with you (oh, yeah, Luke, I'm still waiting on that one), but maybe the reason was something that would have so angered someone that they would have welcomed the chance to frame you.

But why would they have gone so far as to kill Heather? Were they angry at both of you?

And poor Stacy, getting caught up in all of this.

I'm not sure what to believe. You claim innocence and plant enough doubt in my mind to wonder about whether or not you could be, and then you tell me that you were cheating your way through college. It's hard to reconcile those two Lukes, you know?

Or maybe you haven't changed at all.

Audrey

Audrey—

You know, when I got your letter telling me about how you had faith and all that, I was thinking to myself, "Seriously? This girl's a Christian?" You had been so judgmental and showed absolutely no sign of care or compassion whatsoever that I was just really surprised. My first thought was that you were a really big hypocrite.

But when you explained that my letters had thrown you off track and you'd gotten away from what you knew God wanted you to do, until God held a big megaphone up to your ear, that made sense to me. I thought, "Great! She's actually going to be someone I can talk to. Someone who will listen to me. Someone who will encourage me." I was pretty psyched.

So I told you something about who I was. I never said I was proud of it. I never said I was smiling. I never even said I got away with it. You just leapt to a bunch of conclusions and said things to make me feel bad about something that I already felt bad about and then you judged me. Again.

Where is God with His megaphone now?

Luke

Luke,

You're really frustrating sometimes. You know that?

See this whole thing from my perspective. You give me all these reasons why I should believe you're innocent, why you could never do something so morally reprehensible as to murder two girls. I start to think it might be possible, which makes you smile. (That's what you said, Luke!) And then? Then, you tell me that you bought tests in college. You cheated. When I ask you to tell me about yourself, that's the first thing you pull out.

What would you think, if you were in my place?

So, yes, call me judgmental. Call me a hypocrite. I'm showing my compassion by STILL WRITING TO YOU, even as you're giving me more reasons to think that you're not completely trustworthy.

And did you even read all that I wrote about how I'm finally conceding that maybe there's more to the story? My theories about someone framing you, someone knowing what you won't tell me about you and Heather

(I'm going to keep on coming back to that, Luke, so save us some time and just tell me already), admitting that you just might have been in the wrong place at the wrong time . . .

That's me trusting you, Luke. Me trusting you. Even after you told me you're a cheater.

Just because I'm a believer doesn't mean I can ignore the truth. You give me cold, hard facts about your life, and yes, I'm going to jump to some conclusions. Any rational, thinking person would do that, and I get the sense that if I'm the only person who believes you and the only person who talks with you, then you need me to be a rational, thinking person, especially if you want me to help you figure this all out.

You failed to mention that even after my conclusions about the kind of person you are (which could be wrong, mainly because you just laid it out there for me and didn't explain any of it, including who you are now and how your life changed after you cheated), I followed that up by reasoning through how you *might* be innocent, even given what you'd just told me.

I know the worst. (I mean, I hope it isn't going to get much worse, Luke. Please tell me that you've told me the worst.) I know the bad stuff. I know the truly awful things about you.

What's that old saying? Innocent until proven guilty? There's enough reasonable doubt in my mind now, after all that you've shared and all that I've thought through, that I can't say with complete certainty that you're guilty.

So there.

Thank you for jumping on me, though. Thank you for making some conclusions about me, too.

You're wrong, though. Because if I was half as awful as you say, would I still be writing to you and trying to figure all of this out?

Audrey

Audrey—

I think we are having some miscommunication. You started out your last letter by saying I should see this whole thing from your perspective. You said you started to think it might be possible that I could never do something so "morally reprehensible" as murder two girls, which as I said, made me smile. All of a sudden, you sound like you are accusing me of lying again! "That's what you said, Luke!"

I was so confused. I thought, *Why did she write that? Of course I said that. I never denied saying that.* So I went back and looked at your letter before that one, and there, you told me to keep on smiling. I thought you were saying that I was being cocky about cheating. I don't remember word-for-word the letter I sent you after that, but I bet I told you that I wasn't smiling, didn't I? I meant that I wasn't smiling about cheating, not that I didn't smile when it seemed like you were actually willing to consider me innocent.

What else have you and I misunderstood about one another and what have we not understood about where the other one was coming from? You asked me to see things from your perspective and all I really wanted to do was shout at you that *you* should try to see things from *my* perspective.

But what it boils down to, Audrey, is that you're not sitting here on death row, innocent of all charges, and I'm not sitting wherever you are, getting letters from a condemned man who everyone in the world thinks is guilty. Ultimately you have absolutely nothing to gain by believing me, and I have everything to gain if you do.

So which one of us really needs to try harder to see things from the other one's perspective? Yeah, that would be me. So here I go.

First of all, I want to make it clear that I have never been proud of the fact that I cheated. If I had been running that 10K, I would have stayed on the course, too. You still would have been last, because I would have beat you, but that's beside the point.

(Okay, now just to be clear, that was a joke. A friendly joke.)

Seriously, though. I do have integrity. The whole reason I went running in the park the afternoon Heather and Stacy were killed was because when I told my coach that I was going to miss practice, he told me that I'd better run, and I promised him I would. I could have blown it off and just lied to him, but I didn't do that. I'm not usually a cheater. The only reason I cheated in chemistry was because I was desperate. I could not figure out how to pass that class, and I couldn't face the consequences if I failed. I know that's not a good reason and I'm not trying to justify what I did. I'm just telling you what happened. You're never going to believe me if you don't know everything that happened.

In my earlier letter, I stopped there because just telling you that much was hard enough. I didn't want to tell you the rest of the story because I really didn't want you to know and because I was worried about how you were going to react. I think I was waiting to tell you the rest until I heard back from you so I could see what you said about just that much, so that I'd know if it was okay for me to go on. I think I wanted to feel like I could tell you anything.

The Tuesday before that awful day, I walked into my lab and Macie wasn't there—our professor was. I didn't know what was up, but I could tell that it wasn't good. We'd never seen him in there before, but he ran the lab all by himself for the whole four hours and we never saw Macie once. It didn't take long for word to get around that Macie had been caught selling copies of his tests.

As soon as I found out, I started to panic. What was going to happen to me? If I went down too I figured that at a *minimum* I was going to flunk the class and if that happened, I was going to lose my track scholarship. For all I knew, I was going to get expelled. I had no idea what was going to happen.

Heather was used to texting me on Tuesday afternoons while I was in lab because Macie had always been pretty slack about stuff like that, but I wasn't about to text Heather with the professor there—especially since I was scared to death that he was going to walk up to me any minute and tell me that the jig was up. My phone kept vibrating, but I ignored it.

By the time lab was over, Heather had texted me like fourteen times and left three voicemails. She was worried about me, but to me it came across as angry. That's how I felt—like she was mad at me. Like not only was I about to get kicked out of college but now my girlfriend was mad at me. That was my perspective.

Have you ever been upset or worried about something and you took it out on someone who didn't have anything to do with what you were upset about? Like when you stub your toe and then you yell at the person who asks if they can help you? That's what I did to Heather. I hadn't told her that I'd been cheating and the last thing I wanted was for her to find out.

I yelled at her. I told her to quit acting like a pest and that I was tired of her smothering me all the time. We went back and forth like that for a bit and I was pretty mean to her, and then finally she asked me if I wanted to break up and I said that was fine with me.

We broke up, and then we made up. And that's the only reason Heather was in the park that day.

So now you know.

Luke

Luke,

I guess we really have been misunderstanding one another. And you're right. I did jump to a lot of conclusions when I heard about the cheating. I'm sorry. As someone who's currently stressing out about finals coming up (ugh!), I can actually understand the panic you probably felt and how you ended up making some poor choices because of it. Failing an important class, losing your scholarship, being expelled—all very scary possibilities.

What ended up happening? Was the professor on to you? I guess there wasn't really enough time for you to get penalized even if he was, huh? Did you get an incomplete for the semester?

That was a pretty bad joke, Luke. Sorry for that. On the off chance that you win your appeal, are you just going to be able to go back to school and pick up where you left off? Or do you think you'll have to reapply, try out for the track team again? Thirteen pounds makes a difference, you know. I probably could have beaten you on that 10K.

That was a joke, too, by the way.

And, hey, for what it's worth, I know that you said Heather forgave you and everything was okay again, but what happened between the two of you, with you losing your temper and taking your stress out on her, is just one of those things. I don't know if you sit around feeling guilty for that. I hope you don't. Relationships are tough. The people we love the most know us the best, and they end up seeing our worst sometimes. Oh, the stories I could tell you about the drama that surrounded all of my high school relationships. I could be a shrieking harpy over the smallest offenses, all because I was stressed out by something completely different. I'll bet you can't imagine that. You know, me flipping out and telling some poor, clueless boy that I was done. Just done.

That's a joke, too, Luke, seeing as how I've written you those same words. At least you just had to read it and didn't have to listen to it in person. Praise God for every blessing, right?

If prison is as lonely as you paint it, though, maybe even having someone like me there to bring the drama every once in a while would be welcome.

I hope this letter at least made you smile for a little while.

And thank you for trusting me. It makes it easier for me to trust you.

Audrey

Audrey—

You? A shrieking harpy? I can hardly imagine.

(I don't have to keep saying "joke" every time, do I?)

And yes, hearing from you every once in a while is very welcome. More welcome than you can imagine, actually. Except for letters from you, the only things I have to look forward to are visits from the chaplain and being allowed to go into the exercise cage five times a week. I usually get the chance to talk with whoever is in the cage next to me and that's always interesting, if nothing else. It sure hasn't helped me stay in shape though. There's nothing like getting out there and running. I remember how I used to complain about it sometimes or not want to run, but I'd give just about anything to be able to go for a run right now. Windy, rainy, freezing, sweltering. Doesn't matter—you definitely wouldn't hear me complaining.

By the way, what are you training for? You said that you did that 10K for training purposes. What are you doing? A marathon? If so, have you ever run one before? I did a half marathon during my freshmen year in college, but I haven't done a full one yet.

Yet . . .

Anyway. You asked what happened about the cheating and if I would be able to go back to school if I were to be found innocent. I did not get caught so I'm sure I could go back, but I wouldn't. If I ever get the chance to go back to school, I'm going to go to UT. If I ever get out of here, I'm going to become a lawyer and then I'm going to become a defense attorney for the state. I'm going to help guys like me get out of places like this.

You said you hoped that I don't sit around feeling guilty about what happened with Heather. Guilt and anger are about all I ever feel. Guilt over the fact that she never would have been in the park that day if it weren't for me, and anger that somebody would kill her for no reason. Kill two people, actually, although I still believe that Stacy was the original target, so I can't really say "for no reason." I am even more certain now that it was someone who knew her. That's why I still really want to talk to Trevor about this and why I'm still hoping that you'll help me. Have you thought about that anymore?

Thank you for writing to me again. I can't wait for your next letter.

Luke

Luke,

A half marathon, huh? That's half admirable, at least. (And I don't have to keep saying joke either, do I?) I'm training for the Houston Marathon. Yes, the full, in all of its sweaty glory. You would think the second week in January would be cool here, but I'm training with the expectation that it'll be nice and balmy even in winter. I just did my 20-mile training run, and it was brutal. Of course, hearing you say you'd run in any kind of conditions if you could makes me feel guilty for taking even the hottest run of my life for granted. Wish I could spring you out of there for just a little while. I'd take you on a run . . . and leave you in my dust. Half-marathoner and all. Ha!

I still think it's a really, really bad idea for me to talk to Trevor about any of this. About the murders, about your questions, and about how I'm writing you. He still doesn't know that, remember? If he found out that we're in touch, he'd probably lose it, and what excuse could I offer for what I'm doing? I'm not even convinced that you're innocent, which leaves a lot of questions about why I'm writing to you in the first place. Questions I can't even answer myself, much less if Trevor was asking them. Because he'll ask plenty if I mention any of this to him.

Seriously, Luke. How would you feel if you had a sister, and she was in this situation?

Besides, I don't know that talking to him will do any good anyway. You've met him, so you probably know that he's not much of an investigative type or even particularly observant, frankly. Someone could have been following Stacy around in plain sight, and Trevor likely never would have noticed, bless his heart. I mean, this is the same man who barely had the grades to get into college. I love him, but if you're looking for someone to be the brains with all these theories you're looking into, he's not going to be much help.

If you weren't the killer, I wonder if the whole point of the murders was framing you and didn't have anything to do with Stacy at all . . .

Audrey

Audrey—

What is *wrong* with you??

You aren't convinced that I'm innocent but you tell me that you're going to be running the Houston Marathon? What if I really was a murderer, Audrey? I'd know exactly when and where to find you! I mean, I know I'm locked up and everything, but that doesn't mean I couldn't have connections! What if I'm right and the person who killed the girls was after Stacy? Stacy was Trevor's girlfriend. You're his sister. What if it all had something to do with Trevor?

I'm not trying to scare you or freak you out or anything, but you need to be more cautious and you need to look out for yourself. I've got enough stuff to worry about without worrying about you, too.

Sorry. Rant over. Just please . . . seriously. You're only nineteen, I know, which means you probably aren't worldly, which is a good thing! But take care of yourself. Don't be so trusting.

And then in the very next sentence I'm going to say that I wish you would trust me. Seriously, I wish there was something I could do to make you believe me, Audrey. That's how I felt when I was trying to convince the police that I was innocent, too—I would have done anything to make them believe me. I even volunteered to take a polygraph. Once I realized that they were focusing their attention on me, I told them to give me one so that they would quit worrying about me and start focusing on the real killer.

But guess what happened? I passed with flying colors. They said it was because I didn't have a conscience. They said that's why lie detector tests weren't admissible in court—because people who don't know right from wrong or lies from the truth will score well on them. Seriously?

Ever since I got back from that run in the park, this has just been a nightmare that won't end.

That day . . . the day of the murders . . . I saw Macie in the coffee shop on campus in the morning. I was really surprised to see her, but we actually sat together and talked for a few minutes about what happened. Turns out that I hadn't been her only "client" and that I hadn't been the only one she'd offered to "help." Apparently she offered her help to the wrong person, because somebody turned her in—evidence in hand. Macie lost her internship and she was going to be moving as soon as the lease was up on her apartment, but she made it clear that she wasn't going to turn me in. She wasn't going to turn in anybody she'd sold tests to.

Suddenly I was free and clear.

After I finished talking with Macie, I called Heather and I told her everything I'd done and I told her why I'd yelled at her. I said I was sorry and I told her that I loved her and I missed her. She wasn't thrilled to hear that I'd cheated, but she told me that she understood and she forgave me and she said she loved me, too. Even though we both had a lot of studying and stuff to do, neither one of us wanted to wait to see each other. What harm could it do to blow off our responsibilities for one lousy afternoon?

When I went for my run in the park that day I was pretty much the happiest I'd ever been in my entire life. I wasn't going to get expelled. I wasn't going to lose my track scholarship. I hadn't lost my girlfriend. Suddenly I had my entire life in front of me again and I actually thanked God and promised Him that I wasn't going to mess up this time.

Then I got back to the parking area. I stopped my watch and looked around and suddenly it was like my life stopped, too. A nightmare started instead.

I appreciate all these alternate theories that you're coming up with, but I still think that whoever it was had something against Stacy. Her injuries were more . . . severe. Like there was anger involved. A lot of anger. Like whoever did it wanted to hurt her even though she was already dead.

Stacy was the first one to get killed. The blood spatter showed that Heather's body had some of Stacy's blood *underneath* it. That means that Heather was still standing when Stacy was shot. Stacy was also raped first. If Heather had been raped first, some of my semen would have transferred to Stacy, but none was found.

Stacy was killed first. She was raped first. She was raped more violently.

Doesn't that sound to you like whoever did it had something against Stacy? Like everything that happened to Heather was done as an afterthought? Plus I've known Heather for years. I knew everything about her. If somebody wanted to hurt her, I would have known about it.

I don't know what else to say. I guess just thanks for listening again. And please be careful, because I really think I'm right.

Luke

Luke,

Wait. You passed a polygraph test?

I haven't been completely honest with you. Well, I haven't lied, but I've not told you some details that might be of use in all of this. I've been using what I know to try to figure things out, but I've gone farther than just what I know.

I've been making some visits to the campus police department to ask some questions.

Now the campus PD is not a full-fledged police force, of course. But they know a few things. Even more helpful, though, is that they aspire to know more than they do, so when I come in, telling them that I'm doing some research for a criminal justice class and looking super cute (because that's just who I am, Luke), they're always talking it up to really impress me, going on and on about forensic evidence, crime scene investigation, blah, blah, blah, lie detector tests—

Yes. Lie detector tests. I've sat there listening to them droning endlessly on and on about these things.

So I know more than your average college kid.

The police were right. If you were a sociopath with no ability to feel any kind of remorse, then passing a polygraph wouldn't have indicated true innocence. But you're not a sociopath. You've written again and again how much guilt you feel for what happened. You obviously regret the tests you cheated on. And if that wasn't enough evidence that you have a heart, you've expressed concern for me and the danger I might be in.

You're not a sociopath. You couldn't pass that polygraph test unless you were telling the truth.

Before I come to any conclusions, I need you to be completely clear with me.

Did you seriously pass the polygraph test?

Audrey

Audrey—

What if I was really just a smart sociopath who knew enough to realize that I needed to be faking remorse? I'm not, but . . . sigh. Just be careful.

Believe me and be careful. All at the same time.

Yes, I really passed the polygraph. Ask one of the rent-a-cops you talked with to call Daniel Heiser at the Sheriff's Department in Cedar County. Have them ask him exactly what the results were.

Luke

Luke,

I believe you.

Audrey

Audrey—

I got your letter last night and all I've done is stare at it. I fall asleep and then I wake up all of a sudden, scared that it was just a dream, and then I stare at it again and convince myself that I'm awake and not dreaming.

I've had it for twenty-four hours now and I finally can admit, *You really did say that.*

I've asked myself a thousand times what you meant by "I believe you." We've misunderstood each other so many times that I'm afraid I'm misunderstanding you again. *She believes something else. She's not talking about you being innocent.* But no matter which way I try to look at this, there is only one conclusion I can come to: you honestly believe that I didn't kill Stacy and Heather.

And if that's what's going on here, then you're the only person on the face of this planet who believes that. Well, besides the killer. And me. So there are three of us. Three people who know the truth.

One of them can't do anything about it because he's on death row. One of them won't do anything about it because he's happy he's not on death row. So that leaves you.

I hate to ask you for anything because you've done so much already. Just hearing from you every week has helped me mentally and kept me from giving up hope and going crazy. And by crazy, I mean literally crazy. You just wouldn't believe what this place can do to a man. So even though I hate to ask, I'm going to. I'm going to ask—if nothing else—will you keep writing and telling me that you believe me? It will keep me sane.

And this is what I really hesitate to ask, but if you're willing to do even more than just keep writing, will you be my hands and feet and help me figure out how to prove to everyone else that I'm innocent?

But no matter what, promise me this: You'll be careful. You'll take care of yourself. You won't take any risks or arouse anyone's suspicion. If the real killer knows that you know the truth, he might come after you. I honestly couldn't live with myself if something happened to you.

Months ago, I wrote to Trevor. I wrote to Stacy's parents and her sister, too. Of course I didn't hear back from any of them. It was stupid of me to think I would—to think that any of them would be willing to give me any kind of information. I was disappointed just the same. But now I realize what a blessing it was. Not hearing from them is what made me keep trying harder . . . it's what made me decide to write to you.

And you have been such a blessing to me. Much more than you'll ever know. Thank you. Please be careful.

Luke

P.S. Does anyone know that you've been writing to me?

Luke,

Yes. I believe you. I think you're innocent. I don't think you killed Stacy. I don't think you killed Heather. I think you're paying for a crime you never committed.

If you need to hear it again and again, I'll keep saying it.

And I'll do more than that.

See, I'm ten steps ahead of you, Luke. Just as soon as I confirmed what you'd said about the polygraph, in addition to the obvious proof that you aren't a sociopath (you can't fake empathy, you know), I was convinced. What kind of person can be convinced that someone was wrongly and unjustly convicted and do nothing? What kind of self-absorbed, narcissistic, pathetic excuse for a person would just stand back and let someone suffer on death row?

Not me.

Just as soon as I sent off my last letter, I got to work. Operation Free Luke. That's what I started calling the file I put together, full of all of your letters, everything I knew about the trial (which wasn't much), and what I knew about Stacy. Like I told you before, we didn't know one another all that well, apart from Trevor. While she was living her life at UT, I was still in high school, so I didn't know a whole lot.

But I knew enough.

Stacy was in a sorority at UT, and sororities there are a huge deal. The sisterhood and all of the friends she had through her sorority were a big part of Stacy's life. And I don't know what kind of college student you were, but I know that now that I'm away at school, I find myself confiding less in my parents and more in my friends. For instance, my parents have no idea that I'm writing long letters to a convict. (Actually, no one knows that, Luke, to answer your question.) If Stacy was anything like me, she probably shared more information about her life, along with anything weird that was happening, with her friends than she shared with her family. So, instead of going to her parents (like you tried), her sister (like you tried), or my brother (like you tried), I decided to go straight to her friends.

I called up her sorority. Just picked up the phone and called them up, pretending to be a high school senior who's, like, totally stoked and, like, super excited about, you know, becoming a part of the sisterhood and, like, having lifelong friends, and—

Yes, Luke. I talked like that. Really played it up. Even told them my name was Lindsay Johnson, so they wouldn't be able to trace me. I was pretty sure they would direct me to the Greek life office, because I'm sure there are all kinds of rules about formal rush and how all the sororities are supposed to get a shot at prospects, but they ate up my act so eagerly that they invited me to the house.

I drove out from Houston, ready to ask all kinds of leading questions. About how my best friend's sister's boyfriend's cousin knew Stacy, that poor girl who was murdered. (Made all that up, Luke. Awesome, huh?) On the way there, though, I started freaking out because all of a sudden I realized that there was a chance one of them might recognize me from one of the games I'd attended when Trevor was playing. Fortunately, once I got there, it was obvious that I'd never seen any of them before so I didn't even have to worry about that. I'd also figured I'd have to work really hard to get them to talk about it, but after I said just a few things, it was like an all-out therapy session. Seriously! Sisterhood is no joke, because those girls are still grieving Stacy like she was their flesh and blood.

And Heather, too.

Luke, you weren't the only one who loved Heather. And you're not the only one whose heart is broken because she's gone. I hope that's some comfort to you, knowing that her memory lives on even now, even if it's just in a house full of sorority girls. They told me about how she had plans to teach kindergarten one day. About how she volunteered at one of the inner-city elementary schools in the area. About how she was so great about helping the new pledges when they'd join the sorority. About how she was involved in community volunteering through UT. About how she was so genuine and kind. About how much she loved you.

They had scrapbooks from years past, of all the formals and parties they had, and they pulled out one from the year Stacy and Heather were killed. They wanted me to see them, to see how beautiful they both were, as they were telling me about how much they all mean to each other as sorority sisters. (They were still recruiting me, of course, even as they were grieving.) I was going along with it, keeping up the act, until they pulled out one particular picture.

It was of Heather. And you, Luke.

Wow. She was gorgeous, wasn't she? Not in a made-up, over-processed, fake kind of way, either. No, she was legitimately beautiful, in a natural and completely radiant way. In that kind of way that makes girls that look like me feel dumpy and odd looking. I'm cute and all, sure, but I'm not a Heather kind of beautiful.

Stunning. She was stunning.

And you, Luke. You're good looking, too!

Well, you were. I mean, I don't know what you look like now. I've seen your mug shot, but it wasn't anything to brag about, you know. And now? Now that you've been living on prison food and not working out? Well, I don't imagine life on death row has done much for you physically. Or mentally.

You know, forget I said any of that. I only bring it up because I was staring at this photograph, realizing that up until that point, I hadn't ever even seen a picture of you pre-conviction! In all this time we've been writing, I haven't looked you up online beyond the trial and what was going on with that. I didn't believe your claims of innocence, so what was the point? As soon as I got back to Houston, though, I changed that. I feel like I'm a Luke Pennington expert of sorts now. I looked up everything that was out there. All that was out there on the trial. All that was out there about your accomplishments on the track team. I even looked up everything out there about you back when you were running in high school.

You're kind of a big deal, you know that? Before the murders, you were going places. It only made me angrier to read about what you'd done and were expected to do, knowing that someone stole this from you.

I'm getting angry just thinking about it.

That said, if that's all I had gotten from my visit to the sorority, it would have been enough. But those girls gave me more. I asked about you and your involvement, and they all said how nice you'd always been and how they had been shocked when all the evidence had come out against you. They said that it was likely that they didn't know the real you, because you were hardly around, seeing as you were at Solberg running track.

But you were totally innocent in their eyes before the DNA evidence came out. Do you know why?

Because they already had another guy pegged for the crime.

Yes, Luke! Another guy!

Apparently, before Stacy met my brother, she'd been friends with this guy from her hometown named Ben. They were close friends, close enough that they'd registered for a lot of the same classes that first year and were always meeting up to study. The sorority sisters told me that he was super smart but a little creepy. Nerdy and just kind of socially awkward, you know? Not creepy as in a psychopath who would've killed her because that guy from Solberg did that, they said.

Except you didn't do that. And Ben just might have.

Why? Because when Stacy met my brother, she kind of ditched Ben. She stopped hanging out with him. I mean, they still saw one another, but they went from spending all their time together to being casual acquaintances almost, because my brother was taking up all of Stacy's time. Her friends confirmed that she was spending every waking minute she could with Trevor. I think she thought Trevor was so out of her league that she had to work to keep him, and she was willing to do anything, even if her avoidance turned Ben into a stalker.

Seriously. The sisters said he was like a stalker, always following her around, trying to get her to be friends with him like she had been before.

They told me that before the DNA proved you were guilty, they thought Ben had followed Stacy to the park that day, seeing an opportunity to talk to her without Trevor around. (Trevor thought he was a creepy stalker, too, the girls told me.)

I was able to get away from the sorority house with that information. (And with the promise of a bid for the fall semester. Again, totally against the rules probably, but yay for me, right?) I also left with Ben's full name and his major.

Chemistry.

Would you believe that Lindsay Johnson, soon-to-be UT sorority girl, is a mess when it comes to chemistry? Would you believe that she's in serious need of a tutor? Would you believe that Ben said, as soon as she found his email address and wrote him, he would be happy to meet with her and discuss tutoring her?

Yes, Luke! I found him and I wrote to him. I'm going to meet up with him.

I'm so excited about this! He fits the profile! He sounds smart enough to have pulled it off! He has a motive!

I have to rush the end of this letter because I've got to get back on the road. Ben arranged to meet me off campus, this afternoon, back in Austin (the mileage I'm putting on my car is insane these days). I'm going to go in as Lindsay Johnson, then just lay it all out there for him, force him into a confession, and get Operation Free Luke taken care of.

Done and done.

Wish me luck, Luke!

Audrey

Audrey—

    What part of BE CAREFUL didn't you understand?? Now I'm sitting here absolutely frantic and I'm going to have to wait *days* to find out if you're okay or not and I can't do anything except pray that you are!
    Write me back *immediately* and don't do anything else or go anywhere else without talking to me about it first.

    Luke

Luke,

Wow. Protective much?

Just picked up your latest letter at the post office. Which means I did something and went somewhere without talking to you first, just like you told me not to do.

Oops!

I'm kidding. A little. I mean, I don't like the idea of you insisting that I report to you on everything (seriously, Luke?), but I get your concerns about this meet-up with Ben. And what's more . . . well, I appreciate it. Kind of.

Just to put your mind at ease, I had a friend who was looking out for me. A cop friend. Jake is one of the guys from campus PD who I met back when this all started and I needed some questions answered about all the stuff you were putting out for me. He's cool, and we went out a few times at the beginning of the semester, so I trust him.

I haven't told him about you or that we're in touch, but he knew I was meeting up with someone connected to my brother. I told him that I was going out of town and that I'd text him when I got there, then text him when I got ready to leave. You know, just so someone would know where I was and would be making sure I got back okay. (Of course, if I'd gone missing, Jake's in Houston, I was in Austin, so . . . okay, maybe it wasn't the greatest idea.)

But I'm safe now, Luke. I was safe the whole time!

Ben met me at a coffee shop about ten minutes from campus. It was a super busy place with lots of people, so it was really safe. As a matter of fact, I almost couldn't find him because it was so packed!

My cover as Lindsay Johnson was blown completely to bits as soon as he saw me.

Remember how I got worried when I was driving to UT that one of the sorority sisters might recognize me? Well, as it turns out I should have been worried that Ben would recognize me, because that's exactly what happened. In fact, I'd met him before. I'd come into town for one of Trevor's games a few weeks before the murders, and Stacy and I had been sitting together in the student section. How was I in the student section, when I wasn't even a UT student? I had Ben's ticket. All the students got free tickets, and Stacy had arranged for us to meet up with him earlier so that I could use his. He had no interest in seeing the game, but he cared about Stacy and wanted to do something nice for her, even if it meant helping out Trevor's sister.

So I'd met Ben before. How did I not remember that? I guess I'm a bit of a ditz, okay? I didn't remember his name, so when Stacy's sorority sisters told me about him, it didn't ring any bells. But when he was staring me right in the face, I remembered him. Finally, right?

Anyway, when I saw him and thought back to that brief meeting, I remembered that it had been a little awkward, watching him and Stacy interact. Like she felt guilty, like he was sad . . . but they weren't enemies. In those few minutes of seeing them together, it was clear that they weren't at odds with each other. Sure, maybe they argued like friends do and they were going through a weird season now that Stacy was spending all of her time with Trevor, but they were still friends. They'd even said something to each other about meeting up that next week so he could help her study for her chemistry.

Well, with that out in the open, he was very curious about why I'd lied and why I'd arranged a meeting with him. Those sorority girls said that he was socially awkward, but the only awkward person at that coffee shop was me, Luke. Here I was, trying to be a smooth investigator, and instead, I was just a bumbling, mumbling idiot. I told him that I was just really missing Stacy and that I'd been trying to talk to everyone who had seen her before she died. You know, to help me grieve. That I felt like I hadn't gotten a chance to say goodbye.

He had tears in his eyes as he listened to me make up this whole story. He said he understood. Told me that two days before Stacy was murdered, he'd spiked this horrible fever and was so sick he couldn't even make it to class. When he didn't show up for the chemistry class they took together, she'd been worried about him. Yes, even when they were arguing and trying to work out their relationship with Trevor in the picture, she still cared about him. She went to his dorm, saw what shape he was in, and drove him to the hospital. He ended up needing an emergency appendectomy. It was a quick surgery, but the recovery lasted longer than it was supposed to because he got a staph infection.

Unluckiest guy in the world. Well, maybe he comes in second when compared to you.

All that said, the guy was at the hospital when Stacy was murdered. He clearly couldn't have done it even if he felt well enough, what with nurses in and out of his room the entire time, documenting his stats on official time sheets.

I asked if he knew of any problems Stacy was having. He said that apart from Trevor (who he clearly didn't like, probably because he had a crush on Stacy) and all that was changing in Stacy's life because of her relationship, he didn't think she was having any problems. But he did add that they were more distant than they had been, and even though they were still friends, he didn't know her as well as he once had.

I'm not even sure what to do with that, Luke. Are we still pursuing the right leads? Do you still think that the murders happened because someone was after Stacy? It wasn't this guy . . . but could there have been someone connected to Trevor who was after her?

Or are we looking in the wrong place?

Could someone have been after Heather? I mean, she was gorgeous, like I've already mentioned. And you were two hours away at Solberg. Could someone have had an unhealthy obsession with her? Was it possible that something was going on with her that you didn't know about? I'm not questioning your relationship or trying to taint your perception of her . . . just asking.

I want to send this on immediately, like you asked me to (demanded that I do, actually), but I don't want to close without asking how you're doing. I know that things don't change much for you there, but I think about you all the time and just keep praying that you won't spend every minute of your life discouraged. I don't know how it could be otherwise, but maybe these letters help.

Write back soon, okay?

Audrey

Audrey—

How am I doing? Well, for one thing I broke down and *cried* when I finally got your letter. I didn't get teary-eyed or sniffle a little bit or anything like that. I bawled like a baby with absolute relief that you were okay. That's how I'm doing.

So call me protective if you want, but I happen to care about you, plus you are my ONLY hope at this point, so yeah. The thought of you going off to meet the person who might have been the real killer alarmed me a tiny bit. So sorry.

And in your next letter you can go ahead and call me rude, because I'm getting ready to be rude.

Going down there to meet with this guy was *stupid*. Yes, that's right, I said it. Stupid. You can't just go off acting on every little impulse that you have! That's something my little sister would do, and she's thirteen. You're nineteen. Stop acting like a child!

This isn't make-believe, Audrey, and you aren't Nancy Drew. There's a real-life killer out there and it's possible that you're in danger because, yes, I still think Stacy was the primary target.

I'd known Heather for years. We talked all the time. She told me everything. There was nothing weird going on at all.

Stacy, on the other hand, had started dating someone who was headed toward playing in the NFL. He was popular, practically famous. Famous people have fans. Stalkers. You mentioned a long time ago that the killer could have been a female, and you're right. That would actually be a good explanation as to why they were raped the way they were. Someone wanted to make it look like rape, but couldn't exactly do it in the traditional way, you know? What if it was some girl who was upset that she wasn't Trevor's girlfriend and that Stacy was? She might have thought to get Stacy out of the way and then she could have Trevor all to herself.

That's why I think you should talk to Trevor, which, you may remember, was what I asked you to do the very first time I ever wrote you and what I've pretty much been asking you to do ever since then. Seriously, you're a lot like my little sister.

I know this is the busiest time of year for NFL players, but surely you are going to be getting together for the holidays or something, right? Just put some feelers out there. See what you can do.

There's something else I was actually hoping you might do for me, too. There are a lot of organizations out there that work to free wrongly accused prisoners—especially those of us who are on death row. I've written to all the ones I can find, but haven't gotten anything positive back from any of them. Since you're all "Project Free Luke" now, maybe you could write or call some of them? Hearing from somebody other than me might help. I kind of doubt it, since the DNA evidence is so stacked against me and until I come up with some way to explain that, I doubt they're going to be willing to take my case. But it might not hurt if you had the time to write to some of them.

I'm going to go now and start counting the days until I get my scathing letter of reprimand from you. But just remember before you send it that I didn't say *you* were stupid, I said that what you *did* was stupid. And even though I also said you were acting like my little sister, you should probably know that I happen to love my little sister very much. Even when she does stupid things.

Luke

Luke,

I'm like your kid sister. Your kid sister who does stupid things.

Nice.

I'll try not to be offended by that and just chalk it up to how emotional you were when you heard that I was perfectly safe. Hey, I even admitted afterward that meeting up with Ben wasn't the brightest idea. No need for you to tell me I'm as mature as a thirteen-year-old.

And Nancy Drew? Well, Nancy Drew would be able to come in and get your butt out of jail, so think about that the next time you want to criticize me.

There. The scathing portion of the letter is now over. Was it too bad?

I really liked your idea about the organizations that might look into helping you. I did my research and made some calls, but you're right—the DNA evidence is a big stumbling block. My brother's fame isn't helping you much either because everyone I've talked to knows about the case, thanks to the little snippets they've done on ESPN about Trevor Rutledge and his triumph over tragedy with his promising new life in the NFL.

They don't know the half of it, Luke.

You don't know this, of course, because you're not getting *People* magazine there in prison, but Trevor has a new girlfriend. Her name is Carrie. He was devastated when Stacy was killed and stayed single for a while. And by a while, I mean a few months. There was no shortage of women who were ready to step in and comfort him in his loss, and the great majority of them were shameless opportunists. Carrie, though, is actually really nice. She followed him when he got drafted, settled in out there, and is supporting herself, not looking for him to take care of her. She's good for him, honestly.

But here's the thing. They knew each other in college. Back when he was with Stacy.

He wasn't cheating. Don't read that into this. But Carrie was there, back when all of this was going on. I wouldn't have thought it worth mentioning, but when you wrote what you did about someone wanting Stacy gone . . .

Well, does it seem strange to you? That he was in love, then met someone and got involved so quickly afterward, with a girl he already knew? I mean, could you ever move on from Heather? You know, if you were still out here in the real world? Seems to me like real love would be something that would be impossible to move on from, right?

Or am I just being naïve, like a thirteen-year-old? Because you said I was as immature as your little sister. Just throwing it out there again in case you forgot what you said.

Audrey

Audrey—

No, I didn't forget, and I doubt you'll ever let me. But listen, with all this talk about sisters (sorority sisters, little sisters), I had an idea. Well actually I have about 30,000 ideas, but here's one that maybe you can act on . . . safely. What about Stacy's sister? I mean her biological sister. Maybe you could try to talk to her. If they were close, Stacy might have said something to her. Her name is Alexis Kemp-Reynolds.

You know who else Stacy might have talked to? Your brother! Are you going to be seeing him over break? How did exams go, by the way?

So I've been thinking a lot about your question . . . about if I could ever move on from Heather. My first thought was "No." But then I really started imagining a future where I wasn't in here, and honestly, things would probably be pretty different.

Here I have no opportunity to develop relationships with anyone (the guy who walks his pretend dog in the cage next to mine during exercise time doesn't count). My relationship with Heather and my memories of her are probably a lot stronger than they would be if I was out in the real world. I'm sure Trevor still has strong memories of Stacy, but he's also got all sorts of new things going on that are competing with those memories. I don't have anything competing with my memories—at least, nothing good. My memories are all I've got.

So I tried to be really honest with myself. I let myself imagine being exonerated. I let myself imagine going to UT and working on a law degree. I imagined getting out into the real world and helping other people and making friends . . . and yeah. I think I could definitely fall in love again. And even though Heather and I never talked about anything like this, I'm pretty sure that she would want me to move on. She'd want me to be happy.

So I don't know that it's too weird that Trevor is dating again, and I don't think it's too weird that he's dating someone he already knew. It would actually make a lot of sense to fall in love with someone who already knew you and already knew what you'd been through since it would be nice not to have to explain all that to someone. If I ever get the chance to fall in love again, that part of it's going to be a nightmare.

But I could be wrong. Here's an idea: ASK TREVOR!
Thanks for everything. Please write again soon.

Luke

Luke,

Merry Christmas! Well, belated Christmas. I'm so sorry that it's taken me so long to write you back, but my parents and I went out to visit Trevor, seeing as how he was playing on Christmas and couldn't make it back to Texas for the holidays. Family trips are full of togetherness, and it was brutal, quite honestly. My mom especially is a control freak. I made a point of getting out every day to get my runs in, not only for the training but also for my sanity. I thought about you while I was out there running, wondering how your holiday was and if they did anything differently in prison to let you celebrate in your own way. I thought about what this holiday must be like for your parents. I thought about you and how you were feeling.

I spend a lot of time thinking about you, though. I almost feel guilty for going on with my life and doing anything else, knowing that you're there, that I'm the only one who can help you at this point, and that you're counting on me. That's why I did such a bad job in my classes this semester, because I'm trying to save your life.

No pressure, right?

Anyway, all that thinking was good because I realized something that I think you missed when you looked over all the evidence, particularly the DNA evidence. Consider this your belated Christmas gift. Or your New Year's surprise.

You said that when you came back from your run on the day the girls were murdered, you weren't able to find your keys. You left them with Heather, but when you found her body, they weren't on her. They were thrown in the underbrush, right?

Well, Heather wouldn't have done that. So it stands to reason that the killer could have taken them and looked in your car to find something incriminating, to use in setting up a scene that would have made you look guilty.

Did you have anything in the car that would have had your DNA on it, particularly your saliva? Like a water bottle maybe?

If you did, that's totally something the killer could have used! They could have used that to put your DNA on whatever he (or she) used in the rape.

Does that make sense? It's a start, right?

But wait, Luke. That's not all! (Does it feel like Christmas now?!)

I saw Trevor over Christmas, obviously. And I talked to him about all of this.

Well, kind of. I didn't tell him that I know you. I didn't tell him about our letters. I didn't even mention your name. I just watched him with Carrie, got to see how happy he is, and told him, really casually, that I was glad to see him healing after Stacy's death. For the first time since she was murdered, he didn't get angry about someone bringing her up. He talked about some of his happy memories. He mentioned how she was stressed that last semester because her grades weren't what she wanted them to be, but for the most part, he only had positive things to say about her. About how excited she'd been when they were on the road to the national championship, about how she'd told him that last sorority formal had been the best night of her life, and how she'd been making plans for the future.

And Carrie? Luke, she was smiling, too. Holding his hand and smiling as he was talking about Stacy, like she wasn't jealous or angry or anything like that. She's just so genuinely good, and I think she loves him. I think she even loves Stacy, given how important she was to Trevor. There's no way she could have been involved.

I asked Trevor some more questions before we left about Stacy and her stress over her grades and if there was a reason why her grades were suffering. And that actually did make him mad. Well, irritated, at least. He told me, "Back off, Nancy Drew" (wow, does that sound familiar or what?), and then my mom jumped in and told me that I'd do well to stop being concerned about Stacy's grades and start being concerned about my own since they're so miserable and blah, blah, blah.

Just as soon as we got home to Texas, I came back to Houston to stay. Sure, there are still a couple of weeks until school starts, and this place is like an eerie ghost town with random weird guys who stayed on campus over the holidays. (Who does that?) But it beats hanging around at my parents' house and hearing more lectures on my grades and my poor study habits. Don't they know that I'm trying to save a man's life here? (They don't, obviously. But still.)

Honestly, though, the real reason I came back was because I wanted to get back to my mailbox.

Pathetic, I know. Ringing in the new year by myself here in an empty apartment. It feels even more pathetic after watching my brother and Carrie over Christmas.

There's a lot to be said for having someone, and I can see how Carrie has helped Trevor to heal from all the grief he's been carrying around from Stacy's death. It's like she's given him a new chance at all that he thought was gone, and I'm so happy for him.

Happy and jealous. Because I'm immature. (Wouldn't you agree?) But can you blame me? My brother's in love, and I'm stuck by myself here on an empty campus, getting ready to ring in the new year with a two liter of Diet Coke that went flat before finals. (I should've thrown it out back then, but I was distracted by the letters I was getting, the trips to Austin, and all of my Nancy Drew shenanigans. And not, as my mother would be quick to point out, studying.)

It turns out, being pathetically lonely gives me more time to help you out. So there's that, I guess.

Happy New Year, Luke. I'm hoping for the very best for you this year.

Audrey

Audrey—

You are a GENIUS!!!

This explains *everything*—not just the saliva, but the plant matter and dirt that they said was from the parking lot at my school and even my hair. It could have come from the car—probably the floorboard. And yes, I had a drink in the car, and guess what?? It's not in the crime scene photos! I never noticed that or thought about it before, but whoever it was took it with them—along with the gun. Don't go all health-crazy on me, but I bought a Coke and a bag of mini donuts on the way down there because I was in such a great mood that I felt like celebrating. I threw the donut bag away in the trash can when I got to the park, but they didn't have a place for plastic bottles, so I just left it in my car. (Hey, I may be a cheater, but at least I recycle.)

This makes so much sense—I can't believe I didn't think that they might have gotten in my car or notice that the drink was gone before. They contaminated the stick or whatever it was and then they used it to rape the girls and get forensic evidence all over the bodies to incriminate *me*!

Before, whenever I thought about my keys, I guess I always kind of figured that Heather had thrown them into the underbrush—like maybe she was afraid that she and Stacy were going to be kidnapped or something and she was trying to keep somebody from being able to drive off with them. But this. This makes much more sense! It explains everything! You're a genius! Have I told you that already??

Of course it doesn't prove anything, but it sure does help explain things. It helps *so* much. Maybe it will help us figure out who did this and why.

My first thought was that maybe you were right—that maybe whoever did this was trying to set me up. But I'm still not convinced about that. It could be that they just wanted to contaminate it with someone else's DNA and stuff and they didn't really care who they framed—just as long as it got the attention off them. If they were after Stacy, they might have purposefully searched the *other* body—Heather's—because they were looking for keys but didn't want evidence from Trevor's car. It would make sense that someone who knew Stacy would recognize your brother's car. The killer may not have even realized that Heather and Stacy had arrived at the park together and they might have thought the other car was Heather's.

I don't know. My mind is reeling. In a great way, though. Merry Christmas and happy New Year to you, too!!

But seriously, Audrey? You're on campus all alone with a bunch of creepy guys? Are you just messing with me or are you trying to finish me off long before my execution date? How about if you stop telling me about any perilous situations you put yourself in until after they're all over? And I'll just lay here and imagine that you're studying hard, safe and sound.

Speaking of studying hard, I really feel bad that your grades weren't great. Please don't let this situation—please don't let me—affect you like this. You need to be safe. You need to study. You need to go find yourself some nice guy to fall in love with and start building a wonderful life. But not that rent-a-cop guy, Jake, okay? I've been meaning to ask you about that. You guys were dating? Is he even allowed to date students? Isn't that illegal—or at least unethical or against the school rules or something? And why can't he get a job as a real cop? He sounds like a loser. You can do better. Trust me.

Go buy yourself some fresh Diet Coke and give yourself a toast (although you know you shouldn't be drinking that crap, right?). Ya done good, Nancy Drew! Thank you so much.

Luke

P.S. Have you tried to talk to Stacy's sister, Alexis? And when exactly is the marathon? Are you ready?

Luke,

I was so happy to get your letter today. I'm happy every time I get a letter from you, but I was downright euphoric today. Why, you ask? Because today was the first day I've left my apartment in a week. Were the creepy campus dwellers just that scary, forcing me into hibernation? Nope, that wasn't it. (And why would you think I'm intentionally making things up to mess with you? These dudes are real!) Did I find a whole bunch of new leads in your case to research online at all hours? I wish. Was I getting a head start on next semester's reading list?

Pfffffttt.

No. I had the flu. The flu to end all flus. I thought I was going to meet Jesus sooner than later because it was just that bad. I spent the first three days throwing up everything I'd ever eaten in my entire life, which was loads of fun, and it kept me from restocking my kitchen after I came back from my trip to see Trevor. Seriously, I came home, wrote that letter to you, then went to bed before midnight, and woke up feeling like death. I hadn't had time to get my life here back to normal before I was too sick to do anything. So by the time I was able to keep food down, I didn't have anything in the pantry apart from running gels. Which I ate. (Hey, no shame in that, right?) I was just lying there on the floor of the kitchen in three-day-old PJ's with a GU packet hanging out of my mouth, thinking that it would only give me 100 calories and I wasn't sure if that would be enough to even get me to my car, much less to the grocery store.

I probably should have stayed at my parents' house.

Oh, well. Live and learn.

It's funny that you mention Jake in your letter because guess who I ended up texting, as I was lying there on the floor? All of my friends are still away for the holidays, and because I haven't made friends with the guys who never ever leave campus, he was the only person I knew who was even in the same zip code. And he's a great guy who would be willing to help a girl out when she's at death's door.

Yes, we dated for a while. No, that's not illegal or even unethical. We went out a few times, which is not like some illicit affair or anything. And he's not a rent-a-cop. He's working campus PD while he goes to school to get licensed as an EMT. Which was quite providential and all, since he was able to take care of me after I texted him and asked him to hook me up with a box of crackers.

"Audrey girl," he said when he came in and saw me, "you need to be hooked up with an IV, not crackers." I guess I looked pretty rough, because after he brought in all the groceries and medicine he'd picked up for me, he made me lie back down on the couch and stayed with me all afternoon, watching movies while I snoozed off and on, just to make sure I was okay.

You're right when you say that I need to find some nice guy to fall in love with and start building a wonderful life, and that's just the kind of guy I want to find. Not Jake specifically, because we weren't right for each other, but a guy like him, who doesn't consider it a wasted day to just come and sit on the couch because he's concerned for me. You probably would have done that for Heather. You probably did do that for her. I haven't ever had any guy do that kind of thing for me or care that much, so it was really comforting. Made me start thinking of how nice it would be to have someone for the long term, you know?

Anyway, at one point during the afternoon, I woke up to find Jake watching me with some concern. I figured it was because I had drool on my face or something (I'm not a pretty sleeper, FYI), but before I could even make an excuse for that, he said, "Who's Luke?" Apparently,

I'm not a quiet sleeper either, and I'd been talking in my sleep. He told me I'd been mumbling "Help Luke" over and over again. I explained it away, pointing to the Star Wars movie he was watching and telling him that I'd likely be calling out for Obi Wan or Han Solo in another few minutes.

I only mention this to let you know that even at death's door, my mind has been on helping you. Compiling evidence, thinking through theories, contacting more of those organizations that don't seem to want to do much to get your case examined again—this is all "Help Luke." I'm telling you that to soften the blow of what I'm about to say.

Luke, I haven't done squat to help you since the last letter I wrote.

To be fair, apart from the sickness, there isn't a lot I can do right now. I tried contacting Stacy's sister at the only number I could find for her, which was a work number, and she's out for the next week because of the holidays. I thought about getting in touch with Heather's friend who gave reporters a statement after your conviction. (What was her name? Madison? Maggie?) But I haven't felt well enough to even look up the article, much less track down a girl who's probably out of town as well with school still a week away.

And, speaking of a week away, I've been stressed out about next week's marathon, which hasn't helped me to help you. That sounds really selfish, me being concerned about a race when you're on death row, doesn't it? But it was one of those things, something I've been looking forward to lately because I feel like I'm running this for both of us in a weird way. Maybe after we get you out of there you can train for your own marathon, huh?

That's just weird, I know. But I think about these things. "What will Luke do when he's free again?" I can picture you running, going back to school, finding some cute girl to love, and going on to save hundreds of guys like you, wrongly convicted guys who are just waiting for someone to believe them.

I love thinking about these things. I love thinking about you, living a normal life and being who God made you to be.

Anyway, the flu completely messed up my taper, so I don't even know how the marathon is going to go now. You once got onto me for sending you the information about how I was running the race, back when I still thought you were guilty, telling me that I needed to be careful about going somewhere where any psychopath could come and get me. You know, because you could have had friends on the outside. (That makes me giggle now. Big, bad Luke, with friends on the outside.)

But as it turns out you were partially right, because I will need to be careful. Careful that I don't pass out! I'm still not eating real food yet. Just subsisting on subpar, bland offerings because I'm afraid I can't handle anything heavier right now. I'm sure you're just devastated on my behalf, since you live on that kind of food all the time now.

I'm being a rotten help these days, huh, Luke?

I've been praying for you, though. In my lucid moments, I've been praying that we'll figure something out and get you out of there. I don't know how or when, but I know that I'm going to keep on working toward that. Making a few Bs instead of my normal As is a small price to pay for a man's freedom, huh? Yes, Bs are horrible grades by my mother's standards. Mine, too. I'm that kind of girl. I'm an English major. You know why? Because English majors go on to be graduate students . . . because they can't get jobs doing anything else. I'm good with that, though, because I love school. All part of my plan!

And getting you out of there has just become part of the plan as well.

Hey, once you're free, you'll have to come out to Houston to say hi. We'll toast each other with Coke because I do indeed love that crap. (No health nut here.)

And bring some mini donuts with you when you come, because I love those, too.

Hope to hear from you soon, Luke.

Audrey

Audrey—

An English major, huh? That explains a lot . . .

When I get out and become a lawyer, maybe you can work for me. Write depositions and all that good stuff. You don't want to be a student forever, do you?

By the time you get this letter, you'll probably have run your marathon. I hope you do really well. I suspect that you'll do fine and that your body will have had plenty of time to recover from this setback before the race—you're young, and young people bounce back fast. Don't apologize for being psyched about it. I'm psyched for you and I can't wait to hear about it.

I will be praying for you, and I want you to know that it means a lot to me to hear that you're praying for me. I don't think anyone else is doing that. Since I've been in here, I've started reading the Bible and I've really been trying to learn more about God and figure out what He's trying to do in my life and everything, so finding out that you've been praying for me was really important to me. I mean, if two years ago somebody had told me that they were praying for me, I would have smiled at them and said thank you, but inside, I would have been rolling my eyes. But now? Well, it just means everything to me, so thank you.

And don't apologize for not getting anything accomplished yet. I completely understand. I have a new lawyer, though, and I'm giving you his name and number. I told him about you and that if you wanted anything he should give it to you. I don't think he believes me any more than my last lawyer did, but he does seem a little more on top of things and competent. Anyway, he probably has some other contact information for Alexis and he might be able to help you get in touch with Michelle, too. His name is Curtis Weaver and his number is 512-555-2232.

Interesting that you're thinking of me even when you're sleeping because I had a dream about you last night. I was running. Kind of in a marathon, but not really, because it was just around this big city block in Memphis, which is weird, because I've never been to Memphis before in my life and I don't even know what it looks like there, but I knew that it was Memphis. You were there, too, which was also weird, because I don't have any idea what you look like either, but I knew that it was you. In my dream, you had blonde hair and dark brown eyes. Is that even close?

Anyway, I was running around this block and getting near the finish line. I've had dreams before where I've tried to run, but my legs always feel real heavy . . . like I'm in quicksand or something. But this time, I was running really fast and I could see the finish line and I knew I was going to make it, when all of a sudden you passed me and both of us were laughing. It was the greatest dream. I was just laughing and laughing and when I woke up I think I was still laughing. I was so happy. It was disappointing to slowly realize that it wasn't real. I tried to go back to sleep so I could get into it again, but sleep is often pretty hard to come by around here and it didn't work at all. Maybe it will come back to me again tonight. That's the first good dream that I have had since all this started over two years ago.

I'm glad Jake was there to take care of you. You shouldn't have to be alone during something like that. Sorry I called him a rent-a-cop. Nothing but hearty best wishes to him from this point on. Seriously though, my heart stopped when you said he asked you, "Who's Luke?" For a fraction of a second I thought you were going to tell me that he'd found the letters I'd sent you while you slept and I was scared that you were going to tell me that he'd talked you out of writing to me anymore and that I was never going to hear from you again. Where are you keeping my letters, anyway? Do you have a roommate? Just something to think about, because I don't think anybody in your life is going to be too excited if they find out you've been writing to me and I really don't want you to stop.

I don't want you to stop praying for me, either. Please don't. And I won't stop praying for you.

Thank you again so much. Don't forget to let me know how the marathon goes!

In Christ,
Luke

Luke,

So I outran you in your dream, huh? That's kind of sad, that you're being beaten by a girl, even in your dreams. Except not, because this girl right here is FAST!

Seriously! Do you know how fast I ran the marathon? Three hours and twenty-four minutes! I spent all of my long runs pacing myself at ten-minute miles because this was my first marathon, and I was going to take it nice and easy, especially after getting so sick last week. Well, once the race started, I went out going way too fast because I was so excited. I could've kicked myself when I was hitting every mile way ahead of schedule just a few miles in, though, because I just knew I wouldn't be able to push through at that pace for the whole thing. But I did! Sure, everything hurt by mile twenty-one, and I'm pretty sure I hallucinated a leprechaun eating a corndog and doing the hula at mile twenty-four, BUT I FINISHED!

Just in case you need proof of my astounding athleticism, I'm including a picture of me with my finisher's medal with this letter. I waited to take this shot until after I got home and got cleaned up, so you're missing the full effect of the race, but there was no way I was sending a picture of myself with pit stains and sweaty hair to you. Just couldn't bring myself to do it, Luke.

And you were partially right. I do have brown eyes, but I'm not a blonde. My hair is brown. You likely pictured me the way you did because your subconscious knows that Trevor is blonde with brown eyes. Of course, he's also six-four and over 200 pounds. I seriously hope I wasn't that big in your dream.

I'm only five-six. And I'm not telling you how much I weigh. You think pit stains and wet hair are personal, but pounds are really crossing the line.

Anyway, so . . . yeah. That's me. Audrey Rutledge. Nineteen-year-old college sophomore. I am young, I suppose, like you said. I'm sorry, are you eighty-nine now or something? I know prison can age you, but you're still young, too, Luke. Young enough that you depress me when you talk like you have no future left to speak of. I much prefer reading about how you're not giving up on getting out.

And speaking of that, I talked with your lawyer. I'm not sure if you've talked to him since then. I was actually really surprised that you trust me enough to give me that information and have him tell me whatever I needed to know. It made me feel like I'm on the team, you know? That we're really going to figure this out now and get you out of there!

Except I think you're right about your lawyer not believing you. But he seems to know his stuff, at least, and when I told him about the drink in the car, he already knew all about it (because you told him, I'm sure) and said he would look into it.

I'm not even sure what that means, honestly. He didn't explain it. He was more interested in telling me about how I can go and visit you. Said it might help cheer you up a little.

Well, I didn't even know that was a possibility! I mean, I know your mom visits, but I thought only family members were allowed. Luke, I can come visit you! How fun would that be? Can I bring you stuff? I don't even know what you're allowed to have. Letters, of course. Pictures, I hope, since I'm sending one with this letter. But how about books? Sermons on CD? Mini donuts and Coke? Wow, there's so much I don't even know about you, but I want to figure it out. What do you like? What can I bring to make your life easier?

All joking about junk food aside (unless you can have it there, and I'm so bringing some when I come if you can), I was just thinking about you last week during church. Our pastor is preaching through James, and he was talking about how the book was written to those who were being persecuted. Their only "crime" was faith in Jesus, so all that they were being forced to endure was totally and completely unfair.

But James was telling them to count it as joy, because as they suffered, God was using even that dismal season of their lives to produce endurance and perseverance in them. They were going through awful stuff, yet James was telling them that it would be for their good, that God would give them wisdom through it, and that their faith would be made stronger because of it all.

It encouraged my heart to hear it, you know. Even though my current "trials" are nothing more than roommate issues (yes, I have one, and, no, she'll never find your letters because she doesn't snoop through my stuff) and Jake, who took that afternoon he took care of me when I had the flu as evidence that I want to be with him again, I was encouraged. I'm not going through much, but even the little that I face on a daily basis that's challenging and trying is working out greater faith in my life.

As I was thinking through all of that, my mind went right back to you, of course. And I thought, "Wow. Luke needs to hear this."

So I could get the sermons on CD and give them to you in person. And pray with you. It would be so awesome, after all these months of praying for you on my own, to be able to pray with you in person.

You tell me when visiting hours are, and I'll be there!

Audrey

Audrey—

Congrats on your marathon time—I'm really happy for you! You would definitely have beaten me because I probably couldn't have even finished. Especially not with the shape I'm in right now. Push-ups, sit-ups, and running in place just aren't cutting it.

Anyway, thanks for the picture. I don't know if that's what I imagined you looked like or not, because now that I *know* what you look like, I can't remember what I *thought* you looked like. Oh well. Point is that it's nice to have a face to go with the letters and I appreciate it. You looked like you were pretty happy with yourself, as well you should be. Are you ever going to run another marathon, or are you happy just to have scratched that off your bucket list?

I can't have CDs or anything like that (plus, I don't have anything to play them on), but thanks for the offer. And I'm not sure why my lawyer told you that you can come visit, because you can't. Only family allowed (and him, of course). Sorry to get your hopes up!

But I read James last night after I got your letter and then I read it again today. My favorite part is about asking God for wisdom. I keep praying that He will give both of us the wisdom we need to figure out who really did this so that I can get out of here. I hate it here. Sorry, but this week has been especially hard and I just want *out*.

I think you're probably right about God using all this to develop my faith. One thing I think God is working on in me is forgiveness. I think that He wants me to be able to forgive whoever really did this. A lot of times I imagine what it would be like if they were caught and I know I'd be excited and relieved to be found innocent, but how would I feel toward them? Toward the person who was responsible for my being in this place for so long? Toward the person who killed Heather? I know we're supposed to forgive, but I don't know that I'd be able to. I'm wondering if maybe God's not going to let me get out of here until I'm able to forgive this person, and then I worry, because I honestly don't know if I can or not.

Anyway, I'm probably depressing you again. Sorry. Let's talk about something else. Like Jake. So now he's harassing you? Can I call him a rent-a-cop again? What is he doing and what are you doing about it? You can't be nice to him, you know. You can't be "just friends." Girls always think that they can still be friends after a breakup, but I promise you that guys aren't thinking that way at all. If he likes you he's going to take any signs of kindness from you as evidence that you want way more than just a friendship. You're better off making a clean break. Tell him if he doesn't go away and leave you alone, you're going to call the real cops. Tell him you've got a friend on death row with contacts on the outside.

Hey, can you do something for me? Would you look up the difference between centipedes and millipedes? The saying is that centipedes have 100 legs and millipedes have 1,000, but I know that's not right. I remember my biology teacher in high school telling us that there's some way to tell them apart, but I can't remember it.

Find out what they eat, too, if you can. I've got a little friend here who showed up and I thought the least I could do is find out exactly what he is and maybe feed him something. I miss the good old days of being able to just whip out my phone and look up whatever I wanted like that. Now I have to wait a week to find out.

Write soon. Thanks again for the letter and the picture.

In Christ,
Luke

Luke,

Well, that's the most random question ever.

Here's what I found out, though. Centipedes have one pair of legs per body segment, and millipedes have two pairs of legs per body segment. They eat really disgusting stuff, so unless you have a bunch of larvae and worms lying around your cell (and, eww, I hope you don't), your little friend will just have to find some sustenance elsewhere.

Just call me Google.

I was glad to get your letter, of course, but I was pretty bummed out to read that you can't have non-family visitors. Can I just pretend to be your thirteen-year-old sister? You know, since I'm so young? If I was sitting with you during visiting hours, I could search for all kinds of random information on my phone for you. We could look up all kinds of creepy crawly bugs. I'd have to close my eyes after searching for them, though, because bugs freak me out. I don't know how you manage to keep from hyperventilating when one crawls into your cell with you.

I don't know how you manage to keep it together even without the bugs.

You said you didn't want to talk about it because you don't want to depress me. Luke, you should feel free to say anything you want to when you write to me. I may not be there with you, going through it, but I'm a good listener. (Or reader, in this case.) If it helps to talk about it, please, just go ahead. If nothing else, it helps me to know how to pray for you.

I've been praying about what you said, about how you didn't know if you'd be able to forgive the real killer. I can imagine, since I have trouble forgiving people who cut me off in traffic. (Houston is a mess, by the way.) And that's such a small thing compared to what you have to forgive.

But you know what I think? If you hold on to unforgiveness, it doesn't punish the person who's wronged you. It only punishes you. Holding that in your heart will just lead to bitterness, and when the day comes for you to be free, God is calling you to really, truly be free. If you continue to hate the person who did this, leaving your cell won't make a difference, because you'll still be imprisoned by your own feelings.

Maybe this is something God's going to work out in you. I'm praying for that. I'm praying it for both of us, because the better I know you, the angrier I am over every day that you're losing in there.

That's not helpful, though. Me, getting angry. So not helpful, I know.

Subject change, then. And I might as well change it to your favorite topic—Jake. Oh, yeah, I can sense some animosity when you talk about him. He's not harassing me, Luke. He's just calling a lot, sending flowers, and writing really sweet notes about how beautiful I am.

Not harassing me.

You're probably right about making things clear, though. It's not fair to him that I'm not more firm on this. I keep telling him that we're just not right for each other, but he keeps telling me he can change my mind. He's just such a nice guy, and I like hearing that I'm pretty, so . . .

Okay, so I need to tell him to stop writing me notes. I know, I know. But I don't think I need to stop being his friend entirely. Men and women CAN be just friends, you know. Look at you and me, after all.

Hey, I've gotta go. I need to squeeze in a run before it gets too dark outside. And to answer your question, about whether one marathon was plenty . . . well, I'm already registered for number two.

Maybe you and I will run number three together. Here's hoping . . .

Audrey

Dear Audrey—

Thanks for the info, but I let Harvey go before I got your letter. I decided that he didn't belong in here anymore than I did, so I let him go during my exercise time. For the guards who are reading this letter, Harvey was a centipede (or maybe a millipede). That's all. Not a fellow inmate or anything.

Speaking of exercise time, that's about the only chance I have for interaction with anyone. We're taken outside and allowed to spend an hour in these big (relatively speaking) cages. We are each in our own cage, but we can talk with inmates in the cage next to ours a whole lot easier than we can talk with the people in the cells next to us.

Remember that guy I told you about who has a pretend dog? (Who am I to judge? I had a pet millipede.) So he was out there the other day at the same time I was, walking his dog, and I showed him your picture. He asked me if you were my girlfriend, and I said, "Yeah."

I figured if he could have a pretend dog, why couldn't I have a pretend girlfriend, ya know? And he commented on how pretty you were and I agreed. (Because you are very pretty. There. Someone told you you're pretty. Get rid of Jake now.) Anyway, I told him how you'd just run a marathon, but then his dog made a mess and he had to go clean it up, so that was the end of that.

That night, I got to thinking about what I'd told him and I couldn't sleep. All night I kept tossing and turning, thinking about how I'd lied to him and about how God didn't want me to lie. So I decided that the next time I see him, I'm going to tell him the truth.

I felt better about it as soon as I decided that, so I'm really going to do it.

Which brings me to this. I don't want to tell you what I'm about to tell you because I'm afraid it's going to blow whatever progress you and I have made, but I want you to know that I lied about something else, too. I lied to you. And before I even tell you what I lied about, I want you to know that I'm sorry. I really am.

The truth is that visitation here isn't just for family members. I told you that because I don't want you to come here. You don't belong in a place like this. I didn't tell you the truth because I knew you'd argue with me (just like I know you're going to argue with me now). But I'm telling you, Audrey: I do NOT want you to come and visit me. I really appreciate the offer, though. It means a lot to me that you wanted to come.

I'm working on forgiving whoever killed Stacy and Heather, so I hope that you'll work on forgiving me. For what it's worth, I haven't lied to you about anything else, and I promise not to lie to you ever again. You're the only friend I have, Audrey, and it was stupid of me to do something that might screw that up. I hope you'll keep writing to me and being my friend. You're the best thing in my life.

Way better than Harvey.

Take care,
Luke

Dear Luke,

I'm not angry about the lie. I'm just hurt.

When you say that you don't want me to come and see you, is it really about how I don't belong there, or is it just because you don't want to meet me? Because if it's the latter, I won't argue with you. I'll just keep on writing to you, keep on trying to find the killer, and keep far away. No problem. Message received.

But if this is some attempt to shield me, then I've got news for you. I'm writing letters to a man on death row. I know all the gory details of the rapes and murders. So guess what? There's no shield in front of me, behind me, or around me. You don't need to hide your reality from me. I'm all up in your reality! I've even been yelled at over this situation.

So, about that. I finally managed to get in touch with Stacy's sister. After a couple of weeks of leaving messages on her work phone, I figured out that she wasn't going to call me back. (No kidding, right?) I also figured that she now knew my cell phone number and was purposely ignoring the calls when they came in. Knowing that she would have to answer me during business hours, I borrowed a friend's phone to call her so she wouldn't recognize the number.

Once she figured out who I was, she didn't have time for chitchat. When I tried to explain that I was Trevor's sister and that I had some things of Stacy's to return to her family (which wasn't entirely true), she let me have it. I think everyone on campus could hear her shrieking over the phone, which was really embarrassing. She said (well, yelled) that she never wanted to hear Trevor's name ever again and that she didn't want to remember any details from the most awful time of her life. Then she hung up on me.

I'm not sure that her anger was really directed toward Trevor, because he loved Stacy, and they were happy together. I think her anger was directed at everyone connected to that time in her life, including me by broad extension. I'd try to call her back, Luke, but I'd like to retain my sense of hearing.

And besides, I think she's a dead end.

That said, I can handle more than you think I can. Please, if that's why you don't want me to come visit you, reconsider. I can hardly stand to think of you there by yourself, day in and day out, without contact with other people. No, the guy with the pretend dog doesn't count. And Harvey doesn't count either. Do you hear yourself, Luke? You named a bug and called it your pet. You need real, live people to come and see you so that you don't resort to fraternizing with vermin! Don't push me away because you think I can't handle it. If that's your reason, then please think it over again.

But if you're saying no because you don't want to see me . . .

Well, then, just say that.

Praying for you,
Audrey

Audrey—

     You think you're all up in my reality, but you're not. You're not even close. You don't have any idea what my reality is like . . . what I go through every day. You think you're going to sit there across from me with your phone and look up centipedes and millipedes for me? The reality is that you wouldn't be allowed to bring anything in with you. *Anything*. Except quarters. You could bring in $20 worth of quarters to buy me stuff from the snack machines, but after you put the money in you'd have to step back and let one of the guards get it after it drops down. You wouldn't be allowed to touch it because both of us are so despicable that we can't be trusted with a bag of Doritos.

     The reality is that we'd be separated by bulletproof glass and we'd talk on a little black phone. Every word we said would be recorded, just like every letter we write is read before the other one gets it. I would be sitting in a cage—a little tiny cage—for you to look at, like an animal on display at the zoo.

     Before I'm allowed out of my cell, I have to take off all of my clothes and get dressed in new ones while a guard watches me. Then I drop down on my knees, put my hands behind my back, and put them through the same little slot that my food and your letters come from. After I'm cuffed, I have to pull my hands back through the slot and get up from a kneeling position with my hands cuffed behind my back. Then they finally open my cell door and take me to the shower or to visitation or wherever I'm going. The reality is that I have absolutely no privacy, but at the same time, I have almost no human interaction. The times I am around other people I'm demeaned and humiliated and treated with absolute disdain. I'm made to feel ashamed and embarrassed every minute of the day.

I wake up at least three or four times every night either because of noise or because of a roll call or because they turn the lights on, or because I'm having a panic attack. I guess that's what it's called. I don't know for sure because I've never had one until I came here, but I wake up and I can't breathe and I want to tear open my chest and I feel so claustrophobic that I want to rip the bars apart and run outside, but I can't and all I can do is sit there and try to talk myself down so that I can breathe again. That's my reality.

When sleep finally does come, I have nightmares. I usually dream about Heather and she's always so disappointed in me. I feel like I've let her down. If I'd been a better person, we never would have had to meet in that park to make up in the first place and she'd still be alive. If I'd been a better person, I would have prayed for her and talked to her about God and I would know where she went after she died.

Please try to understand, Audrey.

It's not that I don't want to see you. It's that I don't want you to see me.

Luke

Dear Luke,

Reality? This is reality.

You, Luke Pennington, are worth more than what you've been forced to believe there in prison.

I'm coming to see you, so I can look you straight in the eyes—even through bulletproof glass—when I tell you that I believe you're innocent. I believe you're more than what you're forced to live.

I believe YOU.

Audrey

Dear Audrey—

    I know you believe me and I appreciate it more than you'll ever know, but I don't want you to come see me. And you *can't* come to see me unless you're on my list of visitors.
    Which you're not.
    Can we talk about something else?

    Luke

Luke,

Not on the list of visitors, huh? Well, that stinks.

But I get it. And, yes. We can talk about something else. How about the weather? That's a safe topic, right? It's balmy. In February. Because Houston. Or how about how my classes are going? Better than last semester, but only because I've run out of leads to follow in your case and have too much time on my hands. Which stinks. Or how about your favorite topic, Jake? He asked me out for Valentine's Day. I told him I couldn't go out because I had to stay at home and write a letter to a friend, detailing everything that I know about centipedes and millipedes. That excuse right there will likely keep him gone for good now, as he thinks it was my way of blowing him off. And I spent Valentine's Day writing you a letter. Lame, I know.

So . . . any of those strike you as fun topics, Luke?

I can't write a letter full of that fluff. You know I can't, not after what you wrote. And while I'll respect your request to stop asking about visiting, I can't ignore all that you wrote about your life and where you are now. You know, emotionally.

It's horrible. How you're living. What you're being forced to endure. If you were guilty, it would be awful enough. But with you being innocent it's just that much worse. I know that you said I don't get it, and I never will get it. You're right. But I can empathize with what you're going through.

And I can set you straight on a few things.

Those nightmares about Heather . . . wow. I know you said earlier that the only good dream you've had there has been about me, but I didn't realize that you're having horrible dreams about Heather. That makes me so angry, like even your subconscious is out to get you, taking memories that should be treasured and turning them into painful thoughts. I mean, dreaming about Heather should be good, right?

You said it's because you think she's disappointed in you. That you feel guilty for what happened. That if you'd been a better person, you wouldn't have blown up at her, you wouldn't have argued, and she wouldn't have even met you in the park that day. And that if you'd been a better person, you would have spent more time talking with her about God, so that you'd be certain now of where she went after she died.

148

Luke, the load of all of that is too heavy for you to carry around. No wonder you're having panic attacks and nightmares! You can't keep blaming yourself. Bad things happened, yes. You made a bad choice and you were angry, and you didn't handle it the right way. But you didn't make anything happen, Luke. Life stinks sometimes, through no fault of our own. It just happens.

You have to stop blaming yourself. If Heather loved you half as much as you loved her, she would never have wanted you to live with this guilt. It's a disgrace to her memory that you would take your grief over losing her and carry it around as self-blame. It's no way to live.

And as much as you loved her, Luke, you couldn't be her savior. From where you sit now, knowing what you know about God and about forgiveness and what it means to live for Him, I'm sure you wrestle with guilt over how you could have better shared that with her so that she would have experienced what you're experiencing now.

But who's to say that God wasn't doing something in her heart already? Who's to say that she didn't have her own moment of knowing Him and trusting Him? I mean, I know you knew her better than anyone, but can you ever really know someone's heart entirely?

Regardless of what you think and what you feel that you could have done, Heather's eternal security wasn't in your hands. It was in God's hands. And He's fair and just, so much more so than we are as people. (Like I have to tell you that, as you sit on death row for a crime you didn't commit.)

You need to be free from this guilt that you're carrying, Luke. Before you can work on forgiving the killer (and you know you'll need to do that), you need to start by forgiving yourself.

How's that for a topic of conversation?

Audrey

Audrey—

I put you on the visitors list.

Luke

Audrey—

Seeing you today was . . . awesome. Seriously, the best thing that's happened to me since, well . . . since a long time ago. Thank you for coming to see me. Thank you for all the junk food!

You probably aren't even on the highway yet—you might not even be out of the parking lot—but I wanted to write to you right away and let you know how much your visit meant to me.

I was very nervous about meeting you, in case you couldn't tell. You could probably see my heart pounding right through my chest. But your smile. The way you looked at me when you saw me for the first time. It was just so genuine. Like I told you, I'm always going to remember your smile.

My lawyer smiles at me. The chaplain smiles at me. But they are the smiles of pity. The smiles of people who have to be there. People who don't want to get too close to me. Why? Because they think I'm guilty? Because they don't want it to hurt too much when I die? All of the above?

But your smile had no pity in it and you didn't have to be here. You wanted to be here and you believe me and you're not afraid of anything. It made me feel calm and like everything was going to be okay. Next time I have a panic attack, I'm going to remember the way you looked at me today, and I think my chest will open right up again.

The best part was when you prayed with me. The chaplain prays with me, of course, but it feels so canned and obligatory—the same thing he says with every other guy in here. I'm not saying his prayers aren't real or that they don't mean anything, but I think he's burned out. Maybe he started doing this because he thought he could do a lot of good, but now he's kind of wondering. You, though. You were so . . . enthusiastic. So hopeful and so real. When you prayed, I felt like God was right there with us.

And now I'm sitting back here in my cell, and it still feels like He's with me. Everything seems different now.

Thank you.

In Christ's love,
Luke

Dear Luke,

So I'm still smiling, even now.

You have no idea how amazing it was to see you. And, wow, I was so nervous. I spent two hours the night before our visit going through my closet, trying to find the perfect thing to wear, which I know is totally silly. What were you going to do? See me sitting there in a bad shirt choice that left me looking washed out, then turn back around and leave? I had junk food. The odds were good that you were going to sit there and talk to me, no matter what I looked like. Of course, I did have the very rational fear that as soon as you sat down across from me, I was going to throw up everywhere. Nervous stomach. What a welcome that would have been! Vomit all over the glass. You wouldn't have even been able to see what I look like had I done that.

And speaking of what we looked like, it was painfully clear to me that you didn't spend any time at all thinking through your wardrobe choices for our visit. Plain is an understatement, but you somehow managed to look more alive than I thought you would. But your haircut. Luke, do you cut your own hair back in your cell? Probably not, since I'm sure they don't hand out scissors or razors either one to men on death row. (Which begs the question . . . how were you clean shaven? You actually looked like you'd cleaned up for me.)

But the haircut. Is that what your hair looked like on the outside? We've got to get you a better style once you're free. Because it's a crime to let your hair look like that.

Ha! A crime. Get it?

I wrote all of that while smiling, of course, because I'm teasing you. (You really do need a different haircut. I wasn't joking about that.) So much gets lost in these letters because we can't actually see each other and because there's still so much we don't know about one another. How we joke, what you find funny, what makes me laugh out loud . . .

Still, though. I feel like we do know each other, better than I ever imagined I could know someone. And you said you'd remember my smile. So picture me doing just that when you're reading this.

Because I'm still smiling even now, even though it's been a few hours since we said goodbye.

I'm already trying to figure out when I can make my next visit.

It might be a while, unfortunately. All of my trips, particularly the ones I'd been making to Austin to meet up with sorority girls and questionable tutors, are on hold for the next few weeks, at least until spring break. When I registered for classes last semester, I didn't realize that I'd signed up for three—yes, three—reading-intensive classes in my major. All old, 18th-century literature, too, so they're not easy, quick reads. I feel like I spend half my time these days with my head in a book, which is hard to do when I'm thinking about your next letter, praying for you, wondering how you're doing, thinking about that haircut of yours . . .

Kidding, of course. Well, it is true that I think about you all the time.

Anyway, I have midterms coming up, and I'm really anxious about one of the classes because I just know it's going to be a tough test for that one. I'm in a study group, which helps, even though it's immensely frustrating.

Why, you ask? Because Jake is in the study group.

Yeah, I know. He's just auditing the class. Just showed up that first week, out of the blue. Classes here are huge, so what were the odds? I think he used his campus PD privileges to look up my schedule, which I would have happily given him had he just asked, then signed up for the class. Now I don't want him to have any of my details. I can't figure out why he's even in the study group since he doesn't have to take tests for the class, but I'm pretty sure it's because it gives him a reason to come over to my apartment and stay late after everyone else has gone home.

It's . . . creepy. And, no, I'm not leading him on. I'm not even letting him tell me I'm pretty!

Does your offer to contact your friends "on the outside" still stand? I think you were joking about that, because after seeing you and your genuine smile and the way your face lit up as we talked about what God is doing . . . I don't think you have it in you to have anything to do with shady people.

Because you're a good guy. A good guy with a bad haircut. (Still smiling!)

Praying for you,
Audrey

Dear Audrey—

What are you, the hair police? If you must know, I have cowlicks. When afforded my regular barber and ample hair gel, I can really make them work for me. Here? Not so much. And as far as shaving goes, we actually *have* to shave. We lose visitation and things like that if we don't. Unless I tell them that I'm Muslim or something and need to grow a beard for religious purposes (which I don't think they'd buy considering the Holy Bible laying on the desk).

You're pretty. You're pretty. You're very pretty. It's time to file a restraining order against Jake. Tell him you have a boyfriend. Show him my mug shot.

Actually, Audrey, I don't really want you to do that. I don't want you to lie. Remember how I told you that I felt like God was telling me not to lie? Well, I don't think He wants you to lie, either. At least not on my behalf. Going to the sorority house and telling them you were thinking about rushing? Meeting up with Ben under the pretense of needing a tutor? I feel really bad that you did those things because of me.

We can do this without lying. I'm confident that we can find out who really killed Heather and Stacy without doing something that God doesn't want us to do. After all, does it make sense to uncover the truth by lying?

I hope this doesn't sound judgmental or like I'm putting you down for what you did. I actually thought you were brilliant and I love that you were trying to help me. It's just that God's been working on my conscience again, you know?

I think about our visit all the time . . . it still lifts my spirits just to think about you. I would love to have you come see me again if you can. Mom came this past weekend and she comes at the same time every month like clockwork, so if you could come some *other* time, that would probably be better. (Unless you want to watch her cry for two hours. In that case, come on ahead.)

My cat died. (And no, I didn't develop an imaginary cat.) We got Mo when he was a kitten and I was in the fifth grade. We were having recess at school and I was on the edge of the playground, near the road, when I saw him. I think someone had dumped him out of their car because he was really little and he was just sitting on the grassy strip between the sidewalk and the street. I was scared he was going to get hit but I knew I couldn't take him back with me to class, so I just scooped him up and walked home. By the time I got to the house, the school had already called Mom. She was there waiting for me and I think she was ready to tan my hide—until she saw Mo. She gave me this look, but I could tell right away that we were going to keep him. She was fun back then, and a lot easier to talk into stuff. That was before Dad left her. She hasn't been much fun since then and I certainly can't talk her into anything anymore. At least not into believing that I'm innocent. I told her all about how my DNA and hair could have gotten all over the crime scene, but it was almost like she wasn't even listening.

Anyway, on Saturday she told me that Mo had died. Some kind of tumor or something. She had to have him put down. She said that it was very peaceful. I think in her own way she was trying to tell me that it's not going to hurt when they strap me down and stick a needle in my arm . . . that it's going to be peaceful. Or maybe she's just trying to tell herself that.

But you know what? I don't care . . . for two reasons. Number one, because I'm not afraid to die, and number two, because I don't think I'm going to die . . . at least not anytime soon.

159

I think I'm going to get out of here, Audrey. Because of you. And anytime I start to doubt that, I just remember your smile and I believe again.

Come see me when you can. And I think you should try to talk to Stacy's sister again, too. But no lying. And study hard. And run hard. And get rid of Jake.

Love,
Luke

Dear Luke,

Okay, so I've finally stopped sobbing enough to write this letter. Why have I been crying?

Mo. Tiny, little kitten Mo, abandoned on the side of the road. And tiny, little Luke, cowlicks and all, cuddling him up and taking him home. I can see it, just like it's a scene from one of those Lifetime Channel movies that I binge-watch (don't judge me), all in soft focus, with emotional music playing in the background. Mo and Luke, buddies through the years, from kitten and boy to cat and man. And now . . .

I'm over here sobbing again now! And I'm not even a cat person!

I'm so sorry for your loss. That probably sounds stupid, because you've experienced far greater loss than the death of a pet, of course, but wow. I'm really feeling it today. Probably because you mentioned how they're going to strap you to a table and put a needle into your arm. They are so totally NOT going to do that, Luke, and I'm kicking my butt back into gear to make sure it doesn't happen. I think that's why I'm so emotional. Just imagining what will happen if we don't figure this out.

That and I'm afraid that you're going to be upset with me after reading about how you want to be completely honest with people as we're figuring out all of this. I didn't lie, Luke. I want you to know that before I explain the rest of it. I didn't lie. You got that? No lies.

I took your advice. Or rather, I listened to the pointed demand you made about getting rid of Jake. He was persistent, as you may have gathered from past letters, and rather than filing a restraining order (was that a serious suggestion on your part?), I figured talking to him very plainly would work. So one night after the rest of the study group left my apartment, I told him we needed to talk. He seemed really excited about this, like maybe I was finally coming around and would take him up on all that he was offering. You know what he was offering? He had a big plan to take me somewhere for spring break. Like, a road trip down to the beach (not Galveston, but a real beach) for a week away. And not the cheap, crummy version of a beach spring break like most college students experience but a classy getaway, with white sand beaches and solitude.

But I'm not that kind of girl. I mean, there's no way I'd go away alone with a guy like that unless we were married. Even with separate rooms and agreement on how we were just friends (something that you've always said Jake couldn't be, and you were right), it just wouldn't look right. I want to honor Christ, and this trip Jake was trying to talk me into . . . I just couldn't do it. I wouldn't be able to do it even if I wanted to spend more time with him, which I don't.

I told him, again, that we just weren't right for each other, citing this whole trip as a great example of why that is. When I met him last semester, he told me he was a believer and seemed so sincere, which is why I had no qualms about going out with him. After a while, though, it became really obvious that our faith was very different. I won't make judgements on his walk with Christ, but I know that I want all of my life to be about living for Jesus, not just Sundays. We were so different when it came to that, which is what I tried to explain to him again.

He just wasn't getting it, though. He kept asking me why, why, why, Audrey? Why?

So, I told him there was another reason that he had to leave me alone. No, I didn't show him your mug shot. I didn't tell him I had a boyfriend. I didn't do any of the things you told me to do and then told me not to do. (Way to be confusing there.)

But, Luke . . . please don't be angry with me. Remember that I didn't lie, okay?

When he asked why, I told him that there was someone else in my life.

He asked for the guy's name. I told him it was Luke. He asked me if Luke was in one of my classes. I told him that Luke doesn't go to class. He asked if Luke was here in Houston. I told him Luke doesn't live here. He asked me if things were serious with Luke. I told him that they weren't yet but that there was definite potential there.

And now . . . now, I'm mortified. Because your insistence on us being honest about everything has driven me to tell you this.

I basically told Jake that I can't be with him because you and I have got something going on. Sure, I left out the part about how you're on death row and this "something" is all news to you (surprise!), but I was completely honest in what I did tell him.

I'm feeling a little more toward you than I was willing to admit to myself before now. Something is definitely going on here, at least on my part.

And, yes, I know that's stupid. Prison. Death row. Totally not Mr. Right. Stupid, stupid, stupid, just like your kid sister. And, well, that makes it even worse. Reminding you of how you have me lumped together with your thirteen-year-old sister. Nice, Audrey.

If I was a normal person, I would crumple up this letter and never send it. But I'm not normal, unfortunately. I took you seriously when you said we need to be honest, and that's about as honest as I can get. And I know you meant honest when dealing with the search for the killer and not verbally vomiting all of my emotions on you and all, but—

I'm beyond mortified now.

Okay, subject change. Whew, right? (No one's more relieved than I am, Luke.) I left a message for Stacy's sister as soon as I read your letter, and I was sobbing on the phone when I left it (thanks to Mo), so maybe there will be better luck with that, huh? I'll take her pity and try talking to her again if you really think it might lead to something.

I also did some searching online last week and found an email address for Heather's friend Michelle. Do you know her? I sent her an email telling her that I had some questions about Heather and Stacy's friendship, but I haven't heard back from her yet. Have you ever thought about things from that angle? That Heather, who I know you knew completely, may have known something about Stacy that would have given her insight into the killer? Maybe Heather said something in passing to one of her friends? Maybe Michelle was a mutual friend of them both? Heather probably wouldn't have talked much about "girl stuff" with you.

I don't know. Let me know what leads you'd like me to follow, and I'll do my best. I just can't handle sitting around doing nothing anymore, thinking about you and . . .

I just want to help. Honestly.

And hey, be kind to your mother. I know she doesn't say the right things when she comes and visits you, but this is harder on her than either one of us can likely fathom. From what you've told me from our first visit, about your dad leaving and how she never seemed to get over it, she's got a tender heart. That's a good thing, Luke. Don't take her tears as a reprimand against you. Just take them as what they honestly are—grief for what she's powerless about, for what she wants to do.

I think she just wants to help you, too.

Maybe she's the person I should be calling, huh? I would come up to talk to her and watch her cry (like you so helpfully suggested), but . . . well, I'm hesitant to visit you again, given all that I just wrote and how I can hardly believe that I'm actually going to mail this letter to you.

Oh, who am I kidding? I'm already trying to figure out when I can get back there.

Stupid. I know.

But that's me these days . . .

Take care,
Audrey

Audrey—

     Has anyone ever told you that you have terrible taste in men? If not, let me be the first. You have terrible taste in men.

     Seriously, Audrey . . . no wonder you've never been in love before. First Jake, and now me? Sometimes you leave me speechless. Except that I'm writing, so I guess that's "wordless" maybe?

     Nothing is "going on"—not on your part . . . not on my part . . . not on anyone's part. You're just thinking about me a lot because you're worried about me and you want to help me (which I appreciate very much). You don't even know me, Audrey. Trust me, you don't have feelings for me.

     It's like that guy from the latest boy-band that my sister has such a crush on. She's convinced that the two of them are destined to be together or something, but she doesn't really know the first thing about him, and if she did, she'd find out that he wasn't really what she wanted after all. Actually, it's been two years since I've seen my sister, so I'd bet anything that the poster of him that was hanging on her wall is gone. I'm sure she's moved on to something else. Like you need to do.

     I don't mean stop trying to get me off death row—please keep that up as long as you are willing—but you have to stop reading more into your "feelings" than what is really there. Don't you have a student union or something at your school where you can go meet a nice, normal guy with a bright future? Isn't there a young singles group at your church where you can hang out with other people who have similar interests as you? I've seen you,

Audrey, and I've heard your voice, and I know what you're like, so unless you smell really bad or something (which is about the only thing about you that I *don't* know), I really have to think that you can do a whole lot better than you've managed so far. Please give it a try. For me. It makes me happy when you're happy, and I would love to get a letter telling me that you've found some nice boy to go out with for pizza and a movie.

Now, onto other things. Michelle was Heather's best friend in high school. She knew both of us. I don't think Heather and Michelle talked a whole lot after they went off to school, but you can call her if you want. I wouldn't tell her that you're corresponding with me, however. She is quite firmly on the list of people who don't believe me, along with my mom. And by the way, I'm very nice to my mom. It's just kind of disheartening to have the person who is supposed to love you more than anyone else in the world *not* believe you about something like this. And I know it's hard on her. I know.

I think it's weird that Stacy's sister won't talk to you. I think it's weird that she got so upset the one time you did talk to her. Keep after her. Where does she work? Could you go visit her sometime maybe?

Did you get signed up for that email thing where they print out your letters and give them to me? I figure it would save at least two days between the time you write me a letter and the time I get it, which would be really nice since your letters are the best part of my time here. But I'm doing good. I was reading Philippians and I came across this today:

I have learned to be content whatever the circumstances. I know what it is to be in need, and I know what it is to have plenty. I have learned the secret of being content in any and every situation, whether well fed or hungry, whether living in plenty or in want.

And I'm working on that. That and forgiveness. And like I said, I think I'm doing pretty good.

Looking forward to hearing from you again. Tell me all about the pizza and the movie. I want details.

Your friend,
Luke

Luke,

You're right. I do have terrible taste in men.

I heard back from Michelle, Heather's friend. I'd left my phone number in the email, but I hadn't expected her to call me. Maybe just a short email or something, you know. But she called a few days after I sent the email, very eager to talk to me about Heather.

She confirmed all the details you told me about how she and Heather were best friends back in high school, how she knew you, and how she thinks you're guilty. I expected her to say that she was as surprised as Stacy's sorority sisters had been to hear the guilty verdict, but she told me she'd had misgivings about you. Oh, you were a great boyfriend in high school, sure, but when it came time to go to college, you just assumed Heather would go wherever you were recruited.

She said when you signed on with Solberg, you just assumed that Heather would follow you there once she graduated. But when that day came, she told you she was going to UT instead. You and Heather had a big fight, according to Michelle, about the future, about how hard this was going to be on you, and about how you couldn't understand why Heather would make plans apart from you.

But I get that, Luke. I would have been upset if the same thing had happened to me. Of course, as you pointed out, I've never been in love and only have crushes on inappropriate and unattainable guys like your sister does, so what do I know, right? But I do think, even in my inexperience, that you were probably right to be upset that Heather had chosen to go elsewhere. Michelle acted like that was selfish on your part, but hello? You had to go where they were paying for your education. I get that. You weren't some crazy control freak. You just wanted to live in the same town as the woman you loved. You're not a jealous psycho. I've got it.

Michelle didn't, though. Once the word got around about the murders and the rumors came out about your fight right before they happened, she took it as confirmation that you were guilty. When I suggested that perhaps someone had been after Stacy instead and that there was reasonable doubt regarding your guilt, she told me that no one would have wanted to kill Stacy, because she was, and I quote, "totally sweet."

So she'd actually met Stacy. She visited Heather at UT. Heather, who you say you knew so well, was still in pretty close touch with a friend you just assumed she'd lost touch with after high school.

All that said, it was a dead end.

I registered for the email system right after I hung up with her. (Which is how you're getting this message so quickly, obviously.) I was determined to get you this as soon as possible, knowing in my heart that you're innocent and that this piece of information about Heather—that there was something you didn't know about her, which meant that you might not know other details about her that would tell you more about the killer—was something that you needed to know immediately. Before I could get the message started, though, someone knocked on my front door.

Jake.

Yes, groan all you want to, but he didn't come to pester me.

He came to warn me.

He's not stupid, Luke. After I gave him that mortifying information that I also passed along to you in my last letter, he was determined to figure out who you were. So he Googled it. Didn't know your last name, of course, but he knows mine. If you Google "Audrey Rutledge Luke," do you know what shows up? Nothing about me, but loads of stuff on you and Trevor.

He knows Trevor's my brother. He knows about all the questions I asked last semester at the campus PD, right when we first met. And he, rent-a-cop that he is, put it all together.

I didn't tell him any details, but do you know the first thing he said to me?

"He's writing you letters, isn't he? Trying to convince you he's innocent, right?"

I told him that it was none of his business but that I'd been looking into the case, that there was something not quite right about the evidence, and that, yes, I believed you were innocent. That I would swear to it. That I was convinced you were paying for a crime you didn't commit.

And do you know what he said to that?

"Men like him? This is what they do. Find some girl to drag into their mess, convince her that they're changed, tell her that it was all a mistake, and use her. Get her to do all the things on the outside that they can't do themselves, like try to fish up evidence to get them cleared. That's what they do. That's what he's doing to you."

I didn't believe him. I mean . . . not really. Not so much that it was going to change anything. You really are innocent, so it wasn't like that, right?

But it made me think. Especially when he told me that what I'd done was stupid.

He's the second man to tell me that. You told me that what I'd done was stupid, back when I met up with Ben.

Call me stupid (again), but I don't much like being told that I don't know what I'm thinking, doing, or even feeling, Luke. I mean, I may not be as experienced as you when it comes to life, love, and loss, but I know what I feel. To dismiss me and tell me that I'm just really confused isn't right.

After Jake left, I kept telling myself that you weren't like those men he'd been talking about. You weren't. You really were a changed man. You really were innocent. You really were walking with Christ. You really did care about me. You hadn't used me. You weren't still using me.

I waited on the email I was going to send you. I went for a run to clear my head, thinking that after I prayed all about it, I would be in a more encouraging frame of mind to email you. On my way back to my apartment, I stopped by my mailbox, where your letter was waiting.

And it was hurtful. So much so that I did something I'd never done with one of your letters.

I ripped it up and threw it away.

Then I went back out and ran another ten miles. Because that's what I do when I'm happy, sad, mad, angry, frustrated, confused, etc., etc. Ten miles. Another ten miles. Run, run, run.

Let me tell you, I was hurting something awful an hour later. My body, most definitely. My head, certainly. And my heart? Yeah, that too.

But I got back home, took a deep breath, put on my big girl pants, and concluded this:

How you feel or don't feel about me matters very little in all of this. Who you really are and what your motivations are in telling me what you're telling me doesn't really mean much. What I feel (and I can feel whatever I want to) isn't even worth noting.

It all boils down to this. If I truly believe that you're innocent, which I do, then I need to help you figure this out. Which I will continue doing.

And that's it.

So keep your suggestions to yourself on how I need to find a "boy" to go and take me out. Just because I'm not dating anyone doesn't mean I couldn't if I wanted to. Plenty of good options out here and more interest than you'd imagine (since you certainly don't think of me like that), so I don't need your advice. And I'm not going to bother emailing you back with all the details.

I just thought there was something genuine going on between us. You said the only thing you didn't know about me was whether or not I smell bad (which I don't, thank you very much), very nearly in the same breath/pen stroke that you told me I don't really know you.

Which is it? Do we know each other or not?

Maybe you are like those men Jake was warning me about. Painting a picture for me of someone else, so that you're actually right when you say that I don't really know you at all.

I'm going away for spring break. I'll write when I can.

Audrey

Audrey—

You know me.

Luke

Luke,

I know you? What does that even mean? What are you thinking? Was I right? Is this all just about me getting you out of jail now? Is that it?

Whatever. Just . . . whatever. I made a promise, and I meant it. I spent my whole spring break pursuing leads, regardless of what you feel or don't feel.

So there.

I started with Stacy's sister, Alexis. And wow, that was a beating.

Because she wouldn't respond to any of my emails or calls, I went ahead and traveled to where she lives so that I could see her face to face and try to convince her that way. No gimmicks this time, just honesty. She works as a realtor, so she was easy to look up online and even easier to locate once I got there. Alexis Kemp-Randolph. Her name and face are literally on billboards in that small town, and she looks so much like Stacy that I was creeped out.

Except she's a whole lot unhappier than I remember Stacy being.

I had to give my name to the secretary at her office. No big deal, of course, except it turned out to be one. I sat there for about fifteen minutes, playing on my phone and waiting, but no one ever came in to call me back to her office.

But you know who came in through the front door, calling my name?

The police! She called the police on me!

As they were escorting me out of the building, I told them that I had a right to be there and that I wasn't doing anything wrong. They told me that "Mrs. Kemp-Randolph" reserved the right to refuse business to whomever she pleased and that she could, in fact, throw anyone off her property.

Well, then.

Anyway, Luke, I'm not sure that I know any more now than I did before. If I can't figure things out better than this, I'm not going to be able to keep my promise to you, and that kills me. I was so discouraged after all of this that I looked up the one person I thought might be able to understand that kind of grief and hopelessness.

I looked up your mom.

I called her and asked if I could meet her, telling her that I'm your friend, which made her start crying. I guess you haven't told her anything about me, because when I told her that I was trying to help you because I thought you were innocent, she seemed so shocked. I told her that I honestly believed you were a good man (despite your intention in originally writing me, which was likely just manipulation, just as Jake said) and that you deserved to live.

She gave me her address through sobs, and when I showed up at your house, she grabbed me up in the tightest hug I think I've ever gotten. Seriously, your mom is strong.

We spent three hours together. We talked about prison, about the trial, about what the appeals process looks like. She doesn't seem to think you're innocent, but she still knows all about what it would take to get your conviction overturned, almost like she's been hoping for something like this, despite what she believes to be true about your guilt. We talked about your childhood, about what you were like before, about the things you were going to do with your life, about how fast you were when you ran. We laughed over old pictures. Wow, Luke, you really personified "awkward stage" for a good seven years there, you know? But, I'll admit, you grew out of that rather spectacularly.

Anyway.

Your mom isn't a believer. I know you know this, but I was surprised to discover it myself. I think things like this either drive you closer to God or push you farther away from Him, but your mom seems to be stuck in between, not knowing if she can trust God to get her through what she faces, waiting for you to die.

I shared the verses you'd shared with me from Philippians. But I went beyond what you'd shared. I explained how Paul learned to be content with everything—false imprisonment, loneliness, the threat of death—by realizing this one truth.

He could do all things through Christ who strengthened him.

We attribute that verse to all kinds of crazy things. Passing a test, winning a race, achieving some goal. But the original intent was that we could face the very loss of our lives as we know them through Christ continually strengthening us.

I told her that you're clinging to that promise. I told her that I am, too. And I told her that when she feels hopeless, she should trust that God loves her, He sees what she's going through, and He's going to strengthen her, no matter what comes.

I left before it got dark, just so I could drive back to Houston safely. Your mom tried to talk me into staying the night just to be safe, but I told her I'd be fine. She did send me on the road with all kinds of snacks and the promise that I would text her as soon as I got back to my apartment and locked the doors.

She's a good mom, Luke.

I'm not sure what to do beyond this. I'm feeling a little hopeless myself, you know? But I'm back home now, and I hope you'll get this email tomorrow, if not sooner. (How fast do you get these emails?)

Anyway, I've gotta go. I'm meeting Jake for a late dinner.

Take care,
Audrey

Audrey—

Yeah. You know me all right. Did you know that I was going to smile when you said you were meeting Jake for dinner? That I don't believe you for one minute? That I'm fully aware you just put that in there to drive me crazy?

Since you know me so well, Audrey, how can you not know that I want way better for you than you apparently want for yourself? I just want you to be happy. And safe. And I'd like for you to get me out of here. Is that too much to ask?

Luke

P.S. I thought it was weird before that Alexis wouldn't talk to you, and now that she called the police on you? Well, I think it's even more weird. We've got to figure out a way to convince her to talk to you.

186

Luke,

I did meet Jake for dinner. That wasn't a lie. I'm not playing games like that with you.

I'm not nearly as immature as you think I am.

Audrey

Audrey—

You're not playing games, huh?

Okay. So you met Jake for dinner. But you're not going to tell me anything about it? Until when?

Until I tell you what you want to hear? That I don't want you to see him? That I don't really want you to see anybody?

That would be selfish and unfair, for so many reasons. Not because it's not true, but because this whole situation is such a mess.

Here's an idea. How about if we wait until I get out of here, and then—if you haven't found somebody else by then—we can talk about how you feel about me and how I feel about you? Right now, though, there's no point. Did you know that even if we find out who really did this, I could still be in here for years? Look it up. See how long it takes to release someone who's been falsely convicted.

Is that really what you want? Don't you want a *real* relationship? A relationship with someone who can stroke your hair and kiss your lips and tell you how beautiful you are and how wonderful you smell? A relationship with someone who can go to church with you and stand next to you when you're singing and hold hands with you while you're praying? Someone who can give you a lot more than I can give you as long as I'm here?

Luke

Luke,

I'm not playing games. I went out to dinner with Jake. I did it because he called, after I got home from visiting your mother, and told me that he wanted to apologize for the way he'd blown up at me. Remember that? When he got so upset with me because he figured out that I was communicating with you? He took me out to dinner so he could apologize and tell me that he would stop pursuing a relationship with me if it just wasn't going to happen.

So there. That's it. I wasn't going to hold that information hostage from you. I wasn't going to use it to prompt a confession, reaction, or emotion from you, Luke. I'm not a manipulator, and not everything is about you. Sometimes, going to dinner is just going to dinner. And it was an emotional day for me, after all that I'd been doing for you. It was nice to go out and have dinner with a friend, talking about things that have nothing to do with any of this.

This. Whatever this is.

Because I don't know what it is.

I know what I feel. And your idea, about pretending that I don't feel what I feel until it's convenient for you and me both, is a dumb one, Luke. Yeah, you read that right. It's dumb. Because what I feel is not something I chose to feel. I wasn't out looking for someone to care about like this. And I know you said that I only think about you all the time because I'm trying to save your life, but that isn't what this is. You know it isn't. Saying that I can just find someone different, like you were just some guy who fit a place in my life that I was looking to fill, a place that any guy could fill, is insulting.

Because you're not just some guy. You're you.

There may seem to be no point to all of this talk. I get that. Because what could come of it, right?

Honesty. Being real with each other. Saying what we really mean.

I'm not proposing to you, Luke. Good grief. I'm just saying that I care about you and that if things were very different and you were out here, living a normal life like me, I'd be with you. Every chance I got. Every minute I could grab. Every moment of my life.

I'm not afraid to say what I mean. I'm nineteen, not a child. And a real relationship, like you say you want me to have, happens when people aren't afraid to say what they mean.

If you honestly want the best for me, like you say you do, then you'll at least be honest with me. Because caring about a man who can't be completely honest? That's not what's best for me.

So, tell me, Luke. What's really going on?

Audrey

Dear Audrey—

I know you're not proposing. If you proposed to me, I might actually say "yes," because I know that you would take that very seriously—all the "until death do us part," and everything like that.

What you're asking me to do, however, is a lot harder for me to say "yes" to. You're asking me to give it a try. See how things go. All while I'm in here and you're out there. (And by "it" I mean a relationship. Just so we're perfectly clear.)

Don't think I haven't imagined a relationship with you. I have. A million times. It's nice to think about. It's pleasant. It's gotten me through a lot of hard times.

But if we were to decide to do this for real, then we'd have to imagine the ending, too. We'd have to look past those first few giddy moments of smiling shyly at each other or putting both of our hands up to the bulletproof glass and staring into each other's eyes. Remember how we talked before about perspective? I'm asking you now to look really hard at this thing from my perspective.

The way I see it, one of two things is going to happen. Number one is that the real killer is caught, I'm exonerated, and you and I live happily ever after on all of the compensation the great state of Texas doles out for wrongly convicting me. I love that scenario. That one has also gotten me through some tough times.

But unfortunately, there's another scenario, and that's where I've got a problem. Scenario number two is that things don't work out between us. Both of us know that sometimes things just

192

don't work out in a relationship . . . they just don't. And our relationship would have more than its share of cards stacked against it right from the beginning, so us breaking up is a very real possibility. What happens then? Well, you would go on with your life and meet some nice guy and go out for pizza and a movie like I have suggested.

But what about me? Have you really thought about what that would do to me?

You asked me to be honest with you, and this is me being honest. I have lost almost everything, Audrey, and if I lose anything else, I don't think I'm going to make it.

If you still want me to tell you what's going on, I will. If you want to leave things the way they are, I'm really thankful to have a friend like you.

Luke

Dear Luke,

I get your concerns. I really do. I would probably feel the same if the situation was reversed.

But here's where I would be different.

If I was the one on death row, not sure what tomorrow was going to bring, I'd want what I want while I could still have it. And I'd tell you that you were it, that I wanted you, and that we were going to be together. I would enjoy every moment with you, because that would make me happy, knowing that we were together and you were counting on a future with me.

This is what I'm doing, Luke. I'm counting on a future with you.

I'm serious. Okay?

My only reservation is this: Is it me that you want? Or would any future, with any girl, away from death row be just as good?

You said that you imagine a future with me because it gets you through hard times. Would imagining a future with anyone do the very same thing?

I think I have to know, going into this, that it's me you want.

Is it?

Luke, I want to come see you again. But if this is making things too hard for you and it would just be easier for me to stay away, let me know that, too. I'll understand, and I'll keep searching for the real killer, no matter what.

Love,
Audrey

Dear Audrey—

    If I wanted just anyone, I've had plenty of "anyones" to choose from. Fan mail, Audrey. Tons of it. Okay, maybe not tons, but plenty. It's very strange. I mean, what kind of woman writes to guys on death row? (No offense.)

    But really, there have been a lot. They tell me all sorts of things, and they send pictures . . . Nothing too risqué, because that wouldn't get past the guards, but stuff a whole lot more fantasizable than the one you sent me of you with your medal, if you know what I mean. (And yes, Ms. English major—I know fantasizable is not a real word.)

    I think part of it is because of the celebrity status that your brother brought to the murders, but for whatever reason, I have all sorts of women writing to me—telling me that they believe I'm innocent, telling me that they love me, telling me they want to have my babies.

    Every one of them, Audrey, I've thrown away with my breakfast tray the next morning. Every one of them.

    Well, except for one. There was this lady (I'm pretty sure she's in her sixties or something—really old) who wrote to me because she was praying for me and she crocheted me an afghan. I almost wrote back to her, but in the end I couldn't because I didn't have the heart to tell her that we aren't allowed to receive afghans on death row. (I don't know what she thought I was going to do with an afghan anyway . . . it's sweltering here. Absolutely sweltering. No AC in case you're wondering.) I kept her letter because it was really sweet, but I have thrown out all the other ones as soon as they have arrived.

But I kept each one of the letters you sent me (which I think probably means that I actually care more about you than you care about me since you ripped one of mine up and threw it away). Seriously, though, I have every one of them memorized. Along with your beautiful face.

It's definitely you that I want.

Love,
Luke

P.S. Please don't go to dinner with Jake anymore. Please?

Dear Luke,

Fan mail . . . well, that's creepy.

Granted, you look good, so you've got that
going for you. You're a nice guy, too, but
I doubt any of those skanks (okay I'm sorry
for using that word, but what else would
you call someone who sends suggestive
pictures to a man in prison?) and that
afghan-knitting granny really know that
since you've never written back to them.
Maybe it's the danger of it all, huh? A man
on death row, the ultimate bad boy. Or maybe
it's this idea that they can change you
somehow, because women love a project,
right?

I don't understand either of those
mindsets. I don't think like that at all.

I usually gravitate toward guys who have it
all together, you know? Nice guys who have
a solid five-year, ten-year, twenty-year
plan ahead of them, who've prayed it all up

198

and are trusting God for each day. Guys who hold open doors, bring flowers just because, and are genuine with their compliments. Guys who love serving in church, want a family someday, and have kind hearts.

I think that's the kind of guy you are. There's still a lot we have to learn about each other, isn't there? But I feel like we're in a good place, with what we've got between us right now.

Thank you for all that you said in your last letter and for your honesty. It makes it that much easier to tell you that I definitely want you, too. (And not like those other "women" mean it, either. Just keep on throwing away those letters, will you?)

I was thinking about you the other day. Well, let's just say you were especially on my mind a few days ago. I went to see my academic advisor because it's time to register for next semester already. Here's where I confess my nerdiness to you.

I've been taking eighteen-hour semesters since I got here, and I came in with a semester's worth of college credit, thanks to AP tests and some community college classes I did in high school. That said, I, Audrey Rutledge, college sophomore, am actually a senior. For real. My advisor told me I only have two semesters left and that they're going to be light semesters, twelve hours maximum each term.

He asked me if my plan was still to pursue graduate work, and I surprised both of us when I told him no. Before I could even think too long and hard about how my dream has changed, I heard myself telling him that I really wanted to go to work in a law office, just like you joked that I should. Do you know why I said it? Because in the back of my mind, I was thinking, "Maybe I'll be able to help Luke more if I'm working that kind of job."

As if you'll still be in prison this time next year. Can you even imagine?

Well, don't worry. You won't be. And I'm so confident that you're going to be out of there in less than a year's time that you need to start making plans now. Yes, right now.

So, tell me, Luke. What's the first thing you're going to do when you walk out of prison?

Love,
Audrey

P.S. Can I come visit you this weekend?

P.P.S. I won't have dinner with Jake anymore. I promise.

Dear Audrey—

First of all, you can come visit me anytime you want. Maybe once your lighter schedule kicks in that could be every weekend? Since you and my mom are practically best friends now, it doesn't even matter if you come the same time she's here. You'd better coordinate with her though, because it might be smoother if you both check in at the same time.

Joint pat-down. Bonding time.

Second of all, I really wish I could email you back instead of sending my letters snail mail. Hopefully you'll get this by Friday. If not, I hope you take a chance and come this weekend anyway. I guess I'll just have to wait and see if you show up. There is so much of that here. Wait and see. Waiting and waiting and waiting. Most guys here are just waiting for death.

I'm definitely waiting for something else now.

Third of all, the first thing I'm going to do when I get out of here? Hopefully, kiss you. And hold you. And find out for myself whether or not you smell bad. You said you don't—you'd better not have been lying about that.

Hey, I have a question for you. If you usually gravitate toward guys that have it all together, how come you've never been in love before? How come you never found Mr. Right? It seems to me that if the guys you've dated have been like what you described, then things would have worked out by now with one of them. I'm just wondering. I guess I want to know about your old boyfriends. Maybe I want to learn from their mistakes.

I think I'm the kind of guy you described, Audrey. I can't hold open any doors for you right now or bring you flowers, but I definitely want to. And yes, I want to be a part of a church and I want to trust God with my life. I'm honestly not sure about the family part right now. About bringing kids into this world. When I imagine that, my mind goes to really dark places. That's probably not what you want to hear, but you need to know. At first I thought that when I got out of here everything would just be fantastic for the rest of my life—eternal sunshine, you know? But now I'm not so sure.

During exercise time the other day, I was talking with this guy named Squid. I have no idea why they call him Squid and I wasn't about to ask. Maybe he really likes calamari.

Anyway, Squid is friends with a guy named Calvin who used to be in here until he got exonerated. One of those organizations we talked about used DNA evidence to get him a new trial. So Calvin comes back here and visits Squid every now and then.

Apparently Calvin is pretty messed up from being on death row. Granted he was in here a lot longer than I hope to be—I think like twelve years or something—but anyway, the point is that apparently after you get out it's not really over.

I just want you to know that. I'm probably going to need some serious counseling or something. I wonder if the great state of Texas is going to pay for that or if it has to come out of my compensation packet?

Yet even with all of that, I know you're not going to freak out. As a matter of fact, I can almost imagine the response I'm going to get. I don't know exactly what you're going to say, but I know you're going to build me up and tell me things to make me feel better about all of it and I'm going to believe you. Because I believe what you tell me. I believe in us.

One day, I want to be there for you, too. I want to build you up and make you feel better when things aren't going your way. For now, though, thank you for being that person for me. I can't wait to see you.

Love,
Luke

Dear Luke,

When I asked what you'd do first when you left prison, I thought you'd say something like go for a run, drive out into the middle of nowhere, or (my personal favorite) binge on real Tex-Mex. Because you've got to be missing tacos and enchiladas, right?

But no. You're going to kiss me. That's the first thing you want to do.

I'm good with that.

And now I find myself even more motivated to get you out of there so that we can make that happen. Of course, I'm also more motivated now that I know you're hanging out with a guy named Squid. (I can't even imagine how he got that name. I hate to tell you this, but Calamari consumption probably isn't the explanation.)

I'm thankful that you don't know what the future is going to look like, because I think that shows how aware you already are of the challenges ahead. You know, I'd figured, back when we first started talking and I didn't believe you were innocent, that if you actually did turn out to be innocent and got yourself out of there that you were going to have a hard road ahead of you.

I think counseling is going to be a given, maybe for much longer than you're even anticipating now. What you've experienced and what you're still experiencing is actual trauma, so of course you're going to need help sorting it all out. You probably should have started getting counseling after you found Stacy's and Heather's bodies, but that probably wasn't a priority with the authorities while you were a suspect.

Well, we'll make it our priority once you're out. And I'm going to be there right beside you, as much as you want me to be, to help you work through it. I'll also be there to help you ease back into all that you're missing. Like running. Like being able to go wherever you want to. Like having a phone and easy access to everything again. Like being outside. Going to class.

Catching the newest movie. Kissing. Tex-Mex.

Seriously, you like Tex-Mex, right? Because I don't know if things are going to work out with us if you don't.

Kidding. (But developing a love for fajitas, if you don't already have one, would probably be a good thing to do between now and release day, FYI.)

You asked about old boyfriends and why things never worked out with any of them. The easy answer is that none of them were the right guy, obviously. I was waiting for the right one, and I found him. In prison. (Oh, come on. There's some humor in that, right?)

But the better answer is this—I was too immature. I remember writing you and telling you that I was a little dramatic and screechy once upon a time. (I may have even been dramatic and screechy with you.) Even after I became a Christian in high school, I had the wrong attitude about relationships. I expected guys to be perfect, like I was living in some fairy tale, and when they weren't, I was done.

They were good guys, but they weren't living up to my unrealistic expectations.

The problem wasn't them. The problem was me.

But I feel like these past several months, corresponding with you, have helped me to grow up a lot. I'm not expecting perfection anymore. Not from other people and certainly not from myself.

You know, my family wasn't well off when I was growing up. We weren't poor, but we certainly weren't rich. My dad has his own business, and things have always been shaky with making ends meet. That's why Trevor's success has been such a big deal because someone in the Rutledge family finally has some financial security. My parents were the ones who pushed him to work hard in what he was best at, and football was his thing. Look at how well that turned out, huh?

My thing is being smart and making good grades, and I've worked at it just as hard as I can. It's made me a perfectionist, though, not just in school but in all of life. I started seeing how critical I was when I began writing you letters and you began calling me out on it.

It was really convicting, Luke. God used you to show me some hard truths.

My purpose in life shouldn't be to be perfect. It should be about showing grace, about living God's truth, and making Christ as the center of everything my certain reality.

So I can afford to make mistakes now, and I can be okay when others make mistakes. I'm still going to screw up and probably get screechy now and then (sorry), but I think I'm going to be a better person now, not just a better girlfriend.

All that said, that's why nothing ever worked out before. And that's why things are working out now. That, and I've found the right person.

I'm going to send this now so that they'll hopefully print it and get it to you before I show up for visitation this weekend. I'll make sure I smell amazing, even if you won't know the difference, sitting on the other side of the glass.

Can't wait to see you.

Love,
Audrey

Audrey—

It's silly to write you this since I'm going to see you tomorrow, but I just got your letter, so I'm going to answer it anyway and get it sent out with the morning mail. I'll go ahead and tell you now that I'm going to be more nervous tomorrow than I was the last time we met. I can tell. I'm not sure I'm even going to be able to sleep tonight, so now I'm going to have bags under my eyes in addition to a bad haircut. (That hasn't improved since the last time you were here. I haven't really stumbled upon a way to obtain hair gel or a new barber.)

Yes, you have matured. I can definitely see a change in you since we started writing. (Although you did call my fans "skanks," which honestly isn't showing a lot of that grace you were talking about, but I get where you were coming from. I don't have any room to talk. I kept calling Jake a rent-a-cop.) I guess both of us still have a long way to go. Together, though, right?

But anyway, I was honestly kind of disappointed in your answer to my question about the other guys and those relationships not working out. I was hoping that you were going to say chemistry. Not the kind of chemistry that got me into this whole mess in the first place, but you know. *Chemistry*.

Maybe you can't have that kind of chemistry through letters. Through bulletproof glass. But I kind of think you can.

See you tomorrow.

Love and nerves,
Luke

Luke,

I'm in my car looking up at the prison, and I'm grinning like an idiot.

Though I can't be certain, I think you're probably doing the same. I wonder if you're back in your cell, already counting down the days until we'll be in the visitation room together, smiling at one another again.

It's probably my heart playing tricks on me, but you're better looking than I remembered. Of course, that bruise on your cheek that you wouldn't explain wasn't so attractive . . . but your eyes, your smile, even your bad haircut was just like I remembered.

But different, still. Because things have changed.

I was surprised by my feelings. I mean, I've known what I've felt for a long time, thanks to the letters and the first visit we had, but today, it was more. Sitting there, talking to you, looking at you through that glass . . . wow, Luke, the butterflies were off the charts. I feel all gushy and sappy. I'm pretty sure I've never felt this way before.

If it's like this now, what in the world is it going to be like when we're together, I mean really together, all the time?

I need to close this email. I'm typing it on my phone, sitting here in the parking lot. I could have waited until I got home to write, but I wanted to do it before I forgot—while all the details of today were still fresh in my mind.

Like that's going to happen. I'll remember this day for the rest of my life.

I'll miss you. I'll be back next week.

Love,
Audrey

Dear Audrey—

Yeah . . . we definitely have chemistry. Even through bulletproof glass. I know you felt it, too, I could tell. I am more desperate than ever to get out of here now because I want to be with you all the time. I miss you so much already.

You are beautiful. The whole time you were here, that's all I could think about: how beautiful you are and how I couldn't believe that you're mine.

You are mine, right? We haven't talked about our official status. What are we? We certainly aren't going out . . .

Prison humor.

I hate that somebody else has to read our letters—that what's between us can't be private—but one day when I'm out of here, I'll tell you everything I want to say. I'll whisper it in your ear.

In the meantime, let whoever is reading this know that Luke Pennington is officially asking Audrey Rutledge to be his girlfriend.

I hope you can come back next weekend. I can't wait to see you again.

Love,
Luke

P.S. Praying with you again was awesome. That was the best part. Well, one of the best parts.

214

Luke,

I'm yours. Eagerly, joyfully, completely.

So, there it is. Official. Luke and Audrey, together. Let's take out an ad in the paper!

Except . . . not. Because then I would have to tell my parents. I mean, I want them to know how happy I am, but telling them about you? Actually sitting down and breaking it to them that my boyfriend is in prison? I'm dreading that. I don't know if I should wait a while or if I should do it this weekend.

Yes, Luke. They're coming up this weekend. Why? They're trying to talk me out of staying here this summer.

Maybe I need to back up and explain everything.

Back before we started writing each other, I'd tentatively made plans to head out to Arizona and spend the summer with Trevor. When he got drafted, he started feeling charitable towards everyone, even his little sister. He told me I'd have to come out there and stay the summer, that he could get me a job working in the franchise's office, editing and proofreading press releases. (Or getting coffee and doing grunt work. That's probably more accurate.) His house is huge, so he told me I'd have space to myself and wouldn't have to move back home and spend the summer with our parents, working for my dad.

It sounded so good that I agreed immediately.

I hadn't counted on meeting you. I hadn't counted on needing to be here to help you solve this mystery. I hadn't counted on wanting to spend every weekend visiting you.

I told Trevor plans had changed without giving him any details. He went and told our parents. (Because he's a tattle and a kiss-up.) They called me, wanting to know why I wasn't going and insisting that I move home if I wasn't going to be working in Arizona. I told them that I'm staying in Houston for the summer, even though my roommate is moving out and I'll have to move to a different apartment so I can afford the rent, even though I'll have to somehow get this all done during finals week.

This all sounds rather lame, I'm sure. My drama compared to what you've got going on in the real world.

But can I tell you that it's really stressing me out? There's just a lot going on. I want to be honest with my parents and tell them why I'm staying and assure them that I'll be perfectly safe on my own, but that will involve telling them about you. And when they hear that I'm in love with a man on death row? Yeah, well, they will have lost any confidence in my ability to be safe on my own.

I can understand it from their point of view, of course. But it doesn't change anything about how I feel.

I wish I could ignore finals. I wish I could ignore my parents. I wish I could ignore everything but you, me, and what's going on with us.

Because that's literally all I want to think about, Luke. You and me.

I stay awake at night now imagining what life will be like once you're out of prison. Early mornings, waking up to have my quiet time, then getting a text from you, just as you're finishing up your quiet time. Meeting you downstairs at my apartment, where you've just arrived after getting a few miles' run in since we don't live that far apart. Heading out together for another five miles, then walking the last few together. Making breakfast for you, making plans for our day around classes and studying and work. Kissing you goodbye before you leave, then kissing you hello again when everything is done, and we've got nothing but time. Going out together, wherever we want, to do whatever we want. Discovering parts of the city together, eating at all of the hole-in-the-wall restaurants, and singing along to the radio as we go. Bible study together at our church, hanging out with the other couples in our Sunday school class, just learning about walking with Christ together. Staying in on Saturday nights and watching a movie together, falling asleep in your arms, waking up just to tell you goodnight when you have to leave, letting you know that I'll be counting down the minutes until you're back, until I can see you again . . .

Just like that. Perfect.

Then we'll get married. Luke and Audrey Pennington. Wow.

And life after we say I do will be even better, Luke. Can you even imagine?!

So . . . you've just asked me to be your girlfriend, and I've just told you that I dream about being married to you. Well, I'm nothing if not honest. And it only now hits me that you have plans to go back to Austin after you get out, and I'm here in Houston, and . . .

I'm sure we'll figure it out.

But, yes. I'll be your girlfriend. As if that wasn't obvious by now.

Love,
Audrey

P.S. I'm still visiting you this weekend, even with my parents in town. I'll work something out.

Audrey—

Wow. I'm not sure if you should tell your parents. I think it's going to be a little more involved than just the fact that you're dating someone on death row. You're dating the person who they think killed Stacy. Remember her? Trevor's girlfriend? I don't think this is going to go over well at all. Not at all. What I'm actually envisioning is that they're going to talk you into coming to your senses and I'm never going to see you again. Please don't let that happen. And please don't go to Arizona for the summer. Please. I need you.

A long time ago, you asked me if I could move on from Heather . . . if I thought I could ever fall in love with someone else. I told you that I probably could, but now I *know* that I could, because I definitely have. It might be kind of early in our relationship for me to tell you that I love you, but since you just told me that you dream of being married to me, I guess it's probably not. So, there it is. I love you. I'm going to tell you that in person when you come tomorrow—long before you get this letter—so this won't be news to you at all. So I guess what I should be saying is: I still love you.

I can't wait to see you. Drive careful, be careful, and I'm thinking . . . don't tell your parents. But that has to be your decision. Just know that I love you, no matter what.

Love,
Luke

Luke,

Lockdown! The prison is on lockdown.

What does that even mean?! Has there been a fight? Has someone tried to escape? Are you okay?

I'm freaking out here, sitting at a McDonald's just down the road from where you are. They wouldn't let me in. Lockdown, they said. No visitation, no one in or out, nothing. No word on whether or not you're okay, or if you'll even be able to get this email.

I'm not sure I can handle waiting to hear from you. I really, really needed to see you today, to talk to you, to hear you tell me that everything is going to be okay.

Promise me that you'll write the second you get this. Promise me that you'll let me know you're okay.

Of all the days for this to happen . . . My parents found out about us. I wasn't going to tell them. I told myself that I didn't need to explain everything to them. So when they came to talk me into leaving Houston for the summer, I told them I'd worked out the finances to stay, I already had a job in the city, and that it didn't make any sense for me not to stay. I'm a year away from graduation. It would be more beneficial to look into internships, opportunities, things like that—all the things that parents love to hear about, you know.

They were okay with it. I was shocked. So shocked that when they told me they'd help me pack up to move to that efficiency apartment, I sent my mom to box up my closet, forgetting that your letters are in there, right at the back, in an old shoebox.

I know, right? Why would I let her in there, knowing that she snoops like she does? I was just so happy that they were okay with my change of plans that I didn't even think about what she could find.

Anyway, my mom found it, and in a total invasion of privacy, she opened it up and read the first letter. That's so like her, always in my business. She's like that with Trevor, too, but as I've mentioned before, he's a people pleaser (a kiss-up, in other words) and isn't really that great at thinking for himself, so he has no problem with it.

But I do. And when she confronted me, pulling out all of your letters and asking me all kinds of questions about why you were writing, why I had hidden this from them, and why I hadn't thrown them all away, I grabbed them from her, tucked them back in the box, and told her it was none of her business.

Then, my dad came in, and . . . oh, Luke. Things got bad.

I finally admitted to them that I thought you were innocent. That I had feelings for you. That we were together.

My parents freaked out, of course. Worse than I am right now, thinking about you in danger on lockdown. (Actually, maybe I am freaking out more. What's happening in there?!)

They made a lot of demands, a lot of threats, and a lot of ultimatums. Cut off communication with him or you're not welcome in our home anymore. That kind of thing.

And I told them to leave. I told them that they weren't going to condemn an innocent man to death and they weren't going to force me to do it either. I told them they could leave if they wouldn't hear me out and let me explain who you really are.

They didn't listen, of course. They left. And they weren't gone ten minutes before I got a call from Trevor, who naturally took their side and was furious with me.

He was even more furious with you, as I'm sure you can imagine.

I'm glad you're behind bars, Luke, because I think my giant, NFL star of a brother would hunt you down and kill you with his bare hands if you weren't. So I guess I should be thankful for the lockdown, but no, I'm not.

I'm so scared. I'm so scared that something has happened in the prison and that you're not safe. The panic I'm feeling now reassures me that I did the right thing in telling my parents to go.

Because I love you, Luke. I love you. I know you're innocent, and I'm not one bit sorry if I've lost everything standing up for you and for the truth in your situation.

I love you.

Please let me know you're okay. Promise me you'll write me just as soon as you get this.

Please . . .

Love,
Audrey

Dear Audrey—

I'm sorry about the lockdown. I went from being on this ultimate high, pacing in my cell, waiting for them to come get me to take me to see you, to . . . well to depression. I can't even describe to you how sad and mad I am all at the same time.

I'm fine. Lockdowns happen all the time. They just don't usually happen when my girlfriend is supposed to come visit me. I'm sorry I didn't get to tell you that I love you in person . . . that you didn't get to tell me in person. I'm sorry your parents and your brother are mad at you.

This sucks. I've got to get out of here, Audrey. Figure out a way to talk with Stacy's sister. There's a reason she's so upset. I told you early on that I thought the murders had something to do with Stacy, and the way Alexis has been acting when you try to contact her just further confirms my suspicions. I know she won't answer your calls and I know she called the police when you went to her office, but you're brilliant and I know you can figure something out. You're also beautiful and sweet and mine. I love you. Still.

Love,
Luke

Luke,

I was so relieved to get your letter. Lockdowns happen all the time? Are you telling me everything, or are you leaving out details? What's going on in there, Luke? And that bruise you had the last time I saw you. What's happening?

You're right. We need to get you out of there. We need to figure this out. I can't believe we've let ourselves get so caught up in thinking about a future together that we've stopped trying to find the real killer!

I'm going to talk to Alexis. Since nothing else has worked so far, you know what I'm going to do? I'm going to go back to Stacy's hometown this weekend and sit there, watching Alexis's house until she leaves to go somewhere. Grocery store, work, whatever. I'm going to follow her, get out of my car, and confront her before she can avoid me.

I'm done with her ignoring me. Totally
done.

Pray for me, okay?

Love,
Audrey

Audrey—

    I am definitely praying for you. And worrying. I'm not as worried as when you went to see Ben, but somehow this is worse because I care about you so much more now than I did then.
    You are my world. I love you. Be careful.

Love,
Luke

Dear Luke,

Okay. I'm back. I went to Stacy's hometown, found Alexis's house, and sat there in my car, waiting for her to come out.

I felt like a stalker. Which is exactly what I was. But whatever. I was committed to this thing.

I didn't have to wait long. Alexis saw me sitting out there and stormed right out to the car. I was afraid she was going to call the police—or worse (she could've just reached in through the window and strangled me, you know)—but she did something completely unexpected.

She took a big breath, frowned, and said, "What am I going to have to do to keep you from bothering me?"

I was taken aback by that. I've never met her face to face. The only reason I know what she looks like is because of all those realtor billboards, remember? But she's never seen me. She's obviously looked me up, though, because she knew exactly who I was, that I was the one who'd written her, the one who'd shown up at her office . . .

It was a little scary that she knew more than I did going into this.

But I took her at her word. She said she was willing to do whatever it would take to get me to leave her alone. Done and done. I told her I just needed some questions answered.

I didn't tell her about you. I just went straight to the issue, asking her if there was anything strange going on with Stacy before the murders. She told me there was.

Luke, I don't believe her. There's just no way that she was telling the truth. I don't even want to tell it to you, because I don't want you to even consider it. But that's not fair, and I want to be fair to you.

She told me that Stacy called her, right before she and Heather were killed. Stacy was upset, but she wouldn't give Alexis any details apart from saying that Trevor had done something really bad.

That's it. She didn't get any more information. That was the last time she talked to Stacy.

She said that after the murders, she assumed Trevor was responsible. She felt really guilty that she hadn't pressed Stacy for more information and that she hadn't let the police know about the phone call. She said she'd never trusted him.

But Luke, this is another dead end.

Trevor has an alibi, remember? Half the country was watching that game on television. He couldn't have killed her. There is no way! Apart from that, he's never been in any kind of trouble at all. He's a good guy. And he loved Stacy. Why would a good guy who'd never done anything bad suddenly turn into a monster and rape and kill the woman he loved?

It doesn't make any sense. What do you think?

Love,
Audrey

Audrey—

What do you mean Trevor has never been in any trouble? Your brother himself told the police that he'd made some bad decisions before. He said that's why your mom put that GPS tracker in his car in the first place—so that she could make sure he was where he was supposed to be when he was supposed to be there. He made it sound like he'd just been doing the usual "partying too hard" thing or whatever once he got away to college, and the police apparently didn't question him about it any further, but I'm starting to wonder.

Look. I don't want to upset you, Audrey, but what if Trevor is somehow behind the murders? What if he hired someone to kill Stacy for some reason? What if he was afraid that she was going to go to the police about whatever "bad" thing he did?

I know you don't want to think something like that about your brother, but it's something we have to at least consider. And it would explain everything, to be honest. If Trevor hired someone and told them about the GPS, it would explain how they knew exactly where Stacy was. It would explain why the DNA and plant materials were taken from my car, not his. And it would explain why Stacy was killed first, but Heather's murder almost seemed like an afterthought.

We need to figure out what it was that Stacy was talking about when she told her sister that Trevor had done something really bad and why your mom was tracking him in the first place. Can you access his phone records by any chance? I mean, if he was on your parents' account back then, you might be able to figure out their password and view the records online. If you could get them to my lawyer, he can get them to me. I've got nothing but time on my hands anyway and maybe I can look them over and see something unusual. Try to go back to when he went off to college. I know that's a long time ago and this whole thing is probably a long shot as well, but it won't hurt anything. See what you can do.

And please don't be mad at me for making you consider this. I love you, Audrey.

Love,
Luke

Luke,

What GPS tracker? This is all news to me. Why would my mom have wanted to track him? I mean, she's nosy, sure. But Trevor never got in trouble . . . did he? If he did, how could I not have heard anything about it?

Luke, there's no way that Trevor killed anyone. He just isn't capable of doing that or of hiring someone to do it. No matter what Stacy knew, if she even knew anything bad to begin with, it never would have prompted Trevor to act completely out of character like that.

He didn't do it. He's not responsible.

But something's not right.

All four of our phones are on a family plan. We've had a family plan since Trevor and I were in high school. So I already had access to his online phone records. I've sent off PDFs of them to your lawyer, telling him that you wanted to look into them. I'm not sure what you're going to find, Luke, but I hope it leads you to something other than what you're thinking right now. I hope it doesn't lead you to more evidence against Trevor.

I want you out of prison. I want justice to be served. I want you free, here with me. But I don't want my brother there in your place. Can you understand that, that I want him to be innocent, too?

I'm trusting you, Luke. I love you, and I trust you. Please let me know what you're able to figure out.

I'm not going to sit around and wait helplessly, though. My parents still aren't talking to me. But Trevor will talk to me. I know he will. When I show up in Arizona with no other place to go, all by myself, he'll talk to me. He'll take me in and explain all of this and make it right.

I just booked my flight. I'm flying out next weekend.

Audrey

Audrey—

Are you crazy? Why do you keep doing this to me? I know he's your brother and I know you love him and everything, but do NOT go out there!! Do you understand?! He could be a killer, Audrey. He could have *killed* two girls. Let's figure some stuff out and think about this rationally before you do anything else. We'll talk about it when you come see me this weekend. We'll make a plan . . . together.

The first thing we need to talk about are the phone records you sent me. There's a lot here and I haven't had a chance to look at everything as carefully as I want to, but before I got too deeply into Trevor's first year at college, I looked around at the time when Heather and Stacy were killed. I figured Trevor might have called a strange number a few times if he really did hire someone to do his dirty work. I noticed that Stacy called your mom a few days before she was killed. Why was that? I mean, I can't find any time that they'd talked before, so why did Stacy call your mom all of a sudden right then?

We also need to figure out a way to get your parents talking to you again. I think we might need them to tell you what was going on during Trevor's freshman year at school. I can't see anything weird in the record, but of course I don't really know what I'm looking for.

We'll talk more about it when you get here Saturday. I love you.

Love,
Luke

Luke,

Trevor didn't kill anyone. I know he didn't, just as surely as I know that you didn't kill anyone.

Please trust me on this.

Stacy did call my mom a few days before the murder. The police looked at Stacy's phone records and asked my mom about it during the investigation. Stacy was trying to find a football card that Trevor was missing from his collection. She wanted to buy it for him for Christmas, but she was double checking with my mom to make sure she was getting the right one. That's why Stacy called her.

I was planning on coming to see you this weekend, but I have an all-day seminar I have to attend. Student financial planning. Exciting, huh? Attendance every year is a requirement for receiving my scholarship, so even though I know everything they're going to say (because I've gone every summer), I still have to be there. It's very frustrating that I'm not able to be with you, especially considering that I won't even see you the next weekend either.

I'm sorry that I'm missing out on visitation. You have no idea how hard it is for me to be anywhere but with you when the weekend comes around. But I have to go out and talk to Trevor about this next weekend. You spent all these months begging me to go and talk to my brother, so you can't complain now that I'm finally going to do it.

I can trust him. And you can trust me.

I love you, Luke. Pray for me.

Audrey

Dear Audrey—

I know you're not going to get this before you leave, and I know that even if you did, it wouldn't stop you anyway, but I wish you weren't going to see your brother. I wish you'd come talk to me instead. I'm worried to death about you now, Audrey. I love you so much and I just want you to be safe. I want to see you. I love you and I am praying for you. Please write me as soon as you absolutely can so that I'll know you're safe. And know that I will be going crazy until I hear from you.

Love,
Luke

Dear Luke,

My heart is just . . . broken. I can't think of any other way to describe what I'm feeling. There's just pain, physical pain, over what Trevor told me.

He picked me up at the airport, just like I knew he would. He was glad to see me, even though he was still frustrated about you and me. He told me so as soon as he saw me, pulling me in for a hug and saying, "For someone so smart, you have terrible taste in men."

Anyway, he didn't take long to get into it with me. He'd met you before, of course, with Stacy and Heather, and he said he had nothing against you back then. You were a decent guy, studied hard, seemed to really care about Heather, and ran all the time. It was actually nice to hear about you from his perspective like that.

Well, for a little while, at least.

Because it didn't take him long to get into everything else. He rehashed all the details of the murders for me, all the horrible stuff from the trial, all that the papers said about you. I listened to him, nodding and agreeing that—yes—it looked really bad.

But then I gave him your side of the story, telling him about things that just didn't make sense. He listened to me then, and, bless his heart, I think it all just confused him.

He's not the brightest guy. I've told you that before. All the information I was giving him seemed to overwhelm him, so I stopped concentrating on what I already know and switched to what I don't understand.

I told Trevor what Alexis said, about how Stacy was upset about something he'd done. She knew something. And about the GPS tracker my parents had put on his car even before then. What was that about anyway? Was it all connected somehow?

I kept talking as we drove back to his house, and he just kept listening and growing quieter and quieter.

And then, his face, his expression . . . changed. I'll never forget it as long as I live, Luke.

He looked scared. My huge, strong, capable big brother looked scared to death.

I was a little scared myself. Not because I thought he'd hurt me. Not because there was a chance that he could have killed Stacy and Heather (although I was beginning to wonder). Not because he didn't say anything at all for the last ten minutes of the drive.

No, I was scared because I knew that he'd done something.

Trevor did something bad, and Stacy knew about it.

Once we got back to his place, he brought my luggage in, dropped it by the door, and went and sat down on the couch. Do you know who was there, just coming out of the kitchen? Carrie, his girlfriend. She was so excited to see me, but when she saw Trevor with his head in his hands, she looked confused.

She didn't know anything either. She was as much in the dark as I was. And as I began to realize just how bad this had to be for Trevor to act the way he was, I felt sorry for her. She's in love with him, and now . . . now everything is going to change.

It doesn't matter now. It won't matter. Because Trevor confessed something to me.

No, it wasn't about Heather and Stacy. This was about something that he had also confessed to Stacy before she was murdered. He'd been living with it for a few years, trying to get past the guilt, but when he fell in love with Stacy, he wanted her to be all in with him. Sharing his story was the final step to letting her completely in.

It's clear he was afraid to tell me, and to tell Carrie, at first. But I told him I was done (which I say a lot, I know) and that I wouldn't let him get any peace until he told me. So he did.

When Trevor was a freshman at UT, he went to a party and had way too much to drink. He drove himself home, and on the way there, he hit a woman with his car. It was dark outside, and she was wearing dark clothes, a situation that would have been hazardous enough if he had been sober, let alone with him drunk.

She was killed instantly, and he panicked, just like any eighteen-year-old likely would. He fled the scene.

It was a hit-and-run.

It's ruined his life. I don't know how he's managed to live a normal life with this always on his mind. His grief over Stacy's death must have made it even worse.

Carrie was upset. I was upset. Trevor was upset. All three of us were a mess, Luke, as he confessed everything.

But you must have been praying for me, because I had the presence of mind to say what needed to be said. I told Trevor he had to go back to Texas and make this right.

And I know you were praying when I said that because Trevor and Carrie agreed with me.

I'm now back in Houston. We flew in together yesterday, and today we're driving up to

Austin so that Trevor can turn himself in. What a train wreck that's going to be, with people all over that town in love with him, sure to recognize him no matter how much we'll try to keep this quiet and fly under the radar.

I just feel numb. I feel empty and hollow. And I want nothing more than to come and see you, to hear you tell me that things are going to be okay.

But they're not going to be okay, Luke. Because all of our work so far hasn't solved the mystery behind Heather and Stacy's deaths.

All it's done is put another man I love behind bars. Sure, Trevor is doing the right and fair thing by turning himself in, but I'm having a selfish moment, wishing for just a minute that someone was here to console me.

I can't come and see you. I have to help Trevor get through this. And what consolation would there be for me in visiting you right now? A glass barrier, you on one side so far away from freedom, and me, with no way of helping you at all.

I love you. I just don't know what to do anymore.

Love,
Audrey

ROOKIE NFL QUARTERBACK ARRESTED

AUSTIN—Rookie quarterback Trevor Rutledge was arrested late yesterday afternoon after he turned himself in and voluntarily confessed to the hit-and-run death of Tracie Ann Watson nearly five years ago.

Until now, authorities have had no leads in the case. Watson's body was found in the middle of Baylor Street in the early morning hours by a passing motorist. She was pronounced dead on the scene, and an autopsy revealed that Watson had been killed instantly after being struck by a vehicle.

While declining to give details regarding Rutledge's confession and subsequent arrest, authorities did confirm that the case would likely have remained unsolved had Rutledge not come forward.

Despite searching for the driver of the vehicle that hit Watson, investigators were unable to find any witnesses or suspects. According to Deputy Rodney Jacobs, the victim was wearing dark clothing and was intoxicated at the time of her death. "We'd always considered that whoever hit Ms. Watson had no idea that they'd struck and killed an individual," Deputy Jacobs told reporters. "One possibility had always been that the victim was passed out in the middle of the road and was never seen by the driver of the vehicle that hit her. Now, however, we know for certain that this was not the case." Trevor Rutledge was a top pick in last year's NFL draft and passed for 3,421 yards with 22 touchdowns.

Dear Audrey—

Remember all those months ago when you told me that I wasn't a sociopath? That people can't fake empathy? I laughed about that because I knew you were wrong, but now I'm starting to wonder. I actually feel empathy for you right now. And I'm not faking this time.

But I was faking it before, Audrey. It was a lie. All of this. Everything I've told you has been a lie. Except for the fact that I get lots of fan mail. That was true. But remember when I said that I threw them all away and that you were the only one I write back to? That was a lie. I write back to all of them. I keep every one of their letters, too, because it's really hard to keep them straight sometimes. Makes it a lot easier to keep track of what lies I've told to who. Or should that be whom? See? I remember that you're the English major. You're the one who will notice something like that. I'm pretty confident none of the other women would bat an eye over a faux pas like that.

But I digress. The point is that when I started writing to you, I never really thought you'd get hurt. At least, not seriously hurt. I never imagined it ending with everything that's happened with your brother. And I actually feel really *bad* about the way this has all turned out. So maybe sociopaths can feel empathy. Or is it psychopaths? I guess I don't really know the difference. Maybe you should have looked that up for me at some point, like you did the centipedes and millipedes.

Anyway, for whatever reason, the kick I got out of stringing you along is completely gone after hearing about your brother, so I won't be writing you anymore. You need to go take care of him and take care of yourself. Don't worry. I've got plenty of other women to lie to and convince that I'm innocent. Plenty to convince that I love them.

So take care, Audrey. While I'll miss hearing from you and seeing you (hey . . . you were one of the few who actually came to visit—thanks for that!), I don't want to see you hurt any more than you already have been. I'm sorry. Or at least as sorry as someone like me can be.

Sincerely,
Luke Pennington

Luke,

You're lying to me. I don't know why, and I don't know how you can manage it. But I know that you're lying to me.

What we have is real. It's always been real. And I don't know why you're trying to convince me otherwise now. I'm not stupid, nor as naive as that.

Are you trying to protect me? Do you know something that's going to hurt me worse than everything else already has?

I don't know, Luke. But with Trevor in jail now, with you still in jail . . . how much worse can it get? If I believed your letter and could, for one minute, fathom that you were lying to me this whole time, telling me you love me to get me to do your bidding, while you've been guilty the entire time . . . well, if I could believe you, then this would be worse—worse than what's happened with Trevor, worse than anything that could happen from here on out.

But I don't believe you.

You love me. You weren't faking it. You still love me.

And you must think (wrongly!) that taking the blame for a crime you didn't commit is your way of loving me, of protecting me, of giving up your freedom to keep me from learning something worse.

I love you, Luke. I love you, and I'm going to figure this out.

Audrey

Luke,

I'm safe. I'm okay. I did something stupid, just like you're always telling me not to, but I'm safe now.

I'm typing this on my phone while sitting at the police station. Your lawyer is on his way. He's an incompetent ninny, Luke, because everything I've just figured out was news to him. Or maybe he's not. Maybe this is just so completely incomprehensible that NO ONE could have figured it out before now.

But he was gasping as I explained it all on the phone to him, as I was driving to the police station with my hands shaking and my heart pounding. He said he'd come be here with me as I give my statement to the police and as they take it from here.

I think I'm in shock. I'm going to need as much counseling as you will after all of this, probably.

We can go to therapy together. Won't that be nice? Bonding while we're falling apart, together?

Yes. Together.

You know who killed Stacy and Heather, and now so do I.

We're getting you out of prison, Luke.

Love,
Audrey

Dear Audrey—

This is not what I wanted, Audrey. I didn't want you to get hurt. I hope you know that when I first wrote to you all those months ago, I had no idea any of this was going to turn out the way it did.

I'm sorry I lied to you in my last letter. It was stupid of me to think that I was going to be able to keep you from getting hurt, but I couldn't bring myself to tell you what I'd figured out. Once I found out about the hit-and-run, I went back and looked at Trevor's phone records from that night. As soon as I saw who he called, I knew.

And now you know, too. My lawyer called and told me about your statement. He's going to come see me tomorrow and let me read a copy. I wish I could see you instead. I love you, and I'm sorry that you're having to go through this. I wish I could be there for you right now. I can't imagine what you must be feeling, but know that I love you.

Love,
Luke

I, Audrey Rutledge, do hereby voluntarily and of my own free will make the following statement without having been subjected to any coercion, unlawful influence or unlawful inducement.

After months of studying the details of Luke Pennington's trial and conviction in the murders of Heather Goodlet and Stacy Kemp, I began to have reasonable doubts as to his guilt. I began talking with people who knew Stacy and Heather, including my own family members, in an effort to find out the truth.

What I've discovered since then I'm now reporting to the police.

Last week, my brother, Trevor Rutledge, turned himself in regarding a hit-and-run accident that took the life of Tracie Ann Watson in Austin. Before that confession, I had no knowledge of the accident or her death. It only came to light as I was trying to find out who killed Stacy and Heather, and as soon as I knew about it, I urged Trevor to go to the authorities right away, which thankfully he did. His quick agreement to own up to a crime that may mean life in prison (or worse, as he waits for his trial to begin) shows that he is now willing to confess to his crime. The fact that he still hasn't admitted to playing a role in Stacy and Heather's deaths likely means that he really and truly is guiltless as far as they are concerned.

Guiltless . . . but connected, unknowingly.

Through records from my family's cell phone plan, I discovered that on the night of Trevor's hit-and-run, he made a call to my mother, Ellen Rutledge. To the best of my knowledge, my father, Stan Rutledge, knows nothing of this call, my brother's crime, or everything that followed. Knowing the relationship between my mother and my brother better than anyone (because she has always treated me the same way), I concluded that she told him not to go to the police. Her priority is to protect her children, even if that means breaking the law or manipulating us. Throughout my life, she has always been an overprotective, heavily involved parent.

That's no crime, so I can't fault her for that. There are other things, though.

I have spoken with Trevor about what happened the night of the hit-and-run. Trevor (per his own confession) experienced great remorse and guilt, but as I suspected, my mother convinced him that no good would come from turning himself in. She convinced him that Ms. Watson was already dead and that his confession would not bring her back to life. She furthermore persuaded him that Ms. Watson was partly if not wholly to blame for the accident—pointing out that she had been wearing dark clothing and was probably under the influence. She even went so far as to suggest that perhaps Ms. Watson had already been dead—hit by another driver long before Trevor's vehicle struck her.

Trevor listened to our mother. He convinced himself that no good would come from turning himself in to authorities. He cleaned up his act, got serious about doing the right thing, and seemed to turn his life around. But he very nearly turned himself in many times. My mother must have sensed how close he was to confessing and ruining his life, because she became even stricter than she'd been on him when he was in high school. How could she police a grown man who was in another city? She installed a GPS tracking device on his car, so she knew where he was at all times. She insisted that he call her on a regular basis to check in. She even made him swear to her, repeatedly, that he would never confess.

Why did Trevor go along with this? He's a people pleaser, always has been. And my mother's manipulation has messed him up. Me, too. I'm hardly able to write all of this out for fear that she's going to come after me with all of her disappointment and passive aggressive chiding.

(Can the state throw in some free therapy for me for all of my hard work? I think I'm going to need it.)

Trevor continued to struggle with this. Until he met Stacy. He was in love. He wanted to marry her. So he told her the one thing that was keeping him from being completely open to her—that he'd killed someone in a hit-and-run. She did the right thing, of course, insisting that he turn himself in, telling him that she would go with him and help him through it, but he told her he couldn't because he'd sworn to our mother that he wouldn't.

Stacy made the mistake of calling my mother to tell her that she also knew about the crime and that she wanted what was best for Trevor, which was to do the right thing and turn himself in.

My mother didn't think that was best for Trevor.

Before any of them could make a definitive move in any direction, Trevor's football schedule got in the way. He had a game in Oklahoma on the weekend of the murders. My parents and I had plans to drive out there for it, but before we left, my mother told us that she wasn't feeling well. Flu season and all. My father and I, not wanting to lose money on the tickets and the hotel rooms, went without her, telling her to rest up in a quiet, peaceful house. We even went to the drugstore and got her some medicine.

She didn't need it, of course, because she didn't actually have the flu.

She followed Stacy to the park where Heather was going to meet Luke, tracking Stacy in Trevor's car. On one of those check-up calls she'd forced Trevor into, he had mentioned, off-handedly, that Stacy was staying in town, that she had a big test to study for, and that he'd given her the keys to his car in case she needed to leave campus.

My mother's plan had been to find her in Austin. To get her alone somehow, where no one would see them. A 9mm my father has owned for years fits the description of the one used to murder Heather and Stacy—the one that's never been found.

When the GPS showed the car heading toward the park, my mother likely took it as a lucky break. More secluded. She followed the car there and probably parked down the road, not wanting to alert anyone to her presence. I suspect she made her way in on foot, discovering when she got there not only Trevor's car but another one that she didn't recognize.

Luke Pennington's car.

My mother probably took this as a lucky break, too.

After watching from a distance to make sure that the girls were alone, she approached them both and shot them without any warning.

She didn't care who Heather was. She just couldn't afford to leave any witnesses.

She had to contaminate the scene somehow, though. Likely wearing gloves, she took both sets of car keys from the girls' jeans. She threw Stacy's textbook and notes into Trevor's car, knowing that if they were on the table it would make it look as though the girls had a completely normal reason for coming to the park. She wanted it to look as though they'd been lured there by the driver of the second car.

So she got into his car.

She took the floor mats from the driver's side and shook them out over the bodies, hoping that the debris would contaminate the scene with forensic evidence that would implicate him. When she went back to the car, she spotted his drink. And she got an idea.

She proceeded to make the scene look as though violent rapes had occurred. This way, the police would automatically suspect that a man had committed the crime. Using a stick she found in the park, she transferred the traces of saliva from the Coke bottle to the girls' bodies as she did her work, never knowing that Luke had just had sex with Heather and that his semen was still inside her. Had she known this, she likely would have started with Heather so that the semen would be inside Stacy as well. As it was, though, she began with Stacy, furious and filled with rage for all that Trevor almost lost because of her.

Once she was done, she took the weapon, the stick, and Luke's Coke bottle and ran back to her car, parked a mile away. About the time she was pulling out of town, Luke found the girls and the scene that was destined to convict him.

He was in the wrong place at the wrong time.

I'm sure my mother didn't wait long to destroy the Coke bottle and the stick. A silencer is in her bedroom closet, tucked away at the very back, with the gun back in the gun safe, right where my father has always kept it.

I know, because I went back to my childhood home earlier today, using the key I've had my whole adult life, and searched until I found them both. My parents are both at work and never knew I was there.

I swear that this statement is correct and without error, to the best of my knowledge.

Audrey Rutledge

MOTHER OF NFL QUARTERBACK TREVOR RUTLEDGE ARRESTED ON MURDER CHARGES

AUSTIN—Ellen Rutledge, mother of rookie quarterback Trevor Rutledge, confessed to the murder of 20-year-old Stacy Kemp and her roommate, 19-year-old Heather Goodlet.

Two and a half years ago, the bodies of Kemp and Goodlet, who were both students at UT, were found shot and raped in a secluded area of Morgan National Park. Luke Pennington, Goodlet's boyfriend, was quickly arrested for the murders after DNA and other forensic and circumstantial evidence led investigators to believe that he had killed the women. Last year, Pennington was convicted of the murders, despite maintaining his innocence. Pennington's current attorney, Curtis Weaver, stated that he expected a quick reversal of the conviction in light of Rutledge's confession. Pennington has been on death row in the Polunsky Unit in Lewiston since his conviction.

Trevor Rutledge, who turned himself in to authorities in Houston on Tuesday, was arrested on charges of second-degree manslaughter in the hit-and-run of Tracie Ann Watson almost five years ago. In a confession released by authorities, Rutledge, then a student at UT, admitted that he had been drinking the evening of the incident. Rutledge stated that he did not call authorities for fear of losing his football scholarship. Ellen Rutledge confessed that when her son called her and told her what had happened, she convinced him to leave the scene of the accident without notifying police.

"She was already dead," Ellen Rutledge explained in a written statement. "What good would it have done to have had two lives ruined?"

Dear Audrey—

I read the statement you gave to the police. I am so proud of you—of how strong you are. I can't imagine what you have been going through and how hard all of this has been on you. I wish I could help you. I wish I could do something, even just hold your hand and stand alongside you.

My lawyer told me that they searched your mother's credit card records and discovered that she bought the silencer the day after Stacy called her. He said that even with the browser history showing that she'd been tracking Stacy the day of the murders and everything that Trevor was telling them, she still kept denying everything until they finally confronted her with the evidence of that purchase.

He also asked me how I knew you. I told him it was a long story. He said I was very lucky to have you in my life. Like I need to be told that. But I don't believe in luck. I believe that God brought us together. That He's going to help you get through this . . . help both of us.

I don't want to get any hopes up, but he really doesn't think it is going to take very long for me to get out of here since your mom confessed, and especially because of all the publicity surrounding the case thanks to your brother's fame. Apparently the ballistics results on the gun are due back in a few days and everything supports what you laid out in your witness statement. You did a great job. Have I told you how proud I am of you?

The guards have been acting different toward me and it makes me think my lawyer might be right—maybe I really am going to be out soon and they know it. I'd love to see you or hear from you before I get out but if I don't, I completely understand. Please don't worry if that doesn't happen.

Just know that I love you and I'm praying for you. And for your dad and your brother and even your mom. All that work I did to forgive whoever actually killed Heather and Stacy, and now? Well, I don't even know what to say. I'm worried. I'm worried whether you're going to be able to forgive her.

I have to go. It's lights out soon and I want this to go out in the morning mail. Who knows? Maybe I'll actually be out before you even get it.

I love you.

Luke

Dear Luke,

They're going to let you out of prison? You're going to be free?

I'm sorry if I'm slow to believe it. Everything else is a wreck right now, and I just keep assuming that something with you isn't going to work out.

That's how life is going.

My father won't speak to me. Well, that's not entirely true. He's spoken to me exactly once since Trevor's confession, his arrest, my mother's arrest, and her confession. Wow, there's been a whole lot of arrests and confessions going on with the Rutledge clan, huh?

He told me that this will end up destroying his business. All that he's worked for and all that he and my mother spent their lives building together.

In addition to losing his wife, he's now going to lose all credibility and integrity in our small town. He'll lose his business. He'll default on his mortgage. He'll end up not being able to retire—ever. He'll lose everything.

I know he's having a hard time working through everything life has just thrown at him. Trust me, I know what that's like.

But do you know what he said to me?

"Was it worth it, Audrey? All that this is going to do to you and me?"

Because as much as Trevor and my mother are going to pay for all of this . . . well, they're guilty, both of them. But my dad and me? We've got to suffer through it along with them, even though we're innocent.

Dad asked me to give him time. To just go away for a while and give him some space. Which is fine. Well, no. No, it's not. Who says that to their kid, Luke? Who cares so little for their own child that they would do that? (You would know what that's like, though, given the way your dad treated you. Has he gotten in touch with you since the news broke? Oh, Luke, I hope so. I hope you've even had the chance to talk to your little sister.)

I came back to Houston, thinking that at least I'd have Carrie around for a while. She was going to stay here with me, in my apartment, until we got a more definitive answer on Trevor and all that's up ahead with his trial.

When I got there, though, I discovered that she'd left a "Dear John" letter. Or, to be more accurate, a "Dear Trevor" letter, with a note to me attached, asking me to give it to him because she didn't have the heart.

Well, neither do I.

So much for loving him. She's going back to Arizona to go on with her life. Without him.

I'm not sure if I can even blame her at this point.

The apartment is lonely. I knew it would be, even back when I signed the lease. But I didn't know then that I'd be cast out from the rest of my family. All my friends from school are gone, too, home for the summer. I wonder if I'll be able to keep the job I'd planned on starting next week, what with all the bad press out there surrounding my name. Word gets around, and though I'm not guilty, I'm guilty all the same, just by being associated with the Rutledge family. I'm also worried about going back to church and if my reception there will be different, even with the people who are supposed to be my brothers and sisters in Christ.

None of them have called me. Not even to check on me once the news broke.

It's pretty lonely around here.

In all this, I'm trying to remind myself that God knows me. He remembers me. He hasn't forgotten me. And His heart hurts for all the sin and loss that's happened.

It's just hard right now.

But you've had it worse. You've had it so much worse in prison, there in your cell, not knowing if you'd ever get out or if you'd die in there.

And now, it's your time to walk away from this whole mess and live a happy life. To move past it all and be who you were meant to be.

I want that for you, Luke. I really do.

I told you earlier that we could go to therapy together, like this was some funny thing we'll look back on and laugh at. I was clearly in shock when I said it, because I'm never going to be able to laugh at any of this, and I'm positive that all the therapy in the world isn't going to help me now.

Beyond the glib joke, I also made a lot of assumptions that turned out to be wrong. Now though, now that the truth has come out, my family is suddenly the reason for everything you've had to go through.

You don't owe me anything now. You never really did.

When you leave prison, you should be truly free, to go wherever you want to and make the life that you want, forgetting everything that's happened before. We never talked through the details of what would happen, if you'd come here to be with me, if I'd go wherever you were going, how we were going to make this work in the real world . . .

But now I'm glad that we didn't make any promises. Because now you're not obligated to do anything.

I love you. I don't regret anything that I've done. I did the right thing, no matter how hard the situation is now. I wouldn't change any of it. I wouldn't change falling in love with you.

But things have changed, nonetheless.

If you got out now and we were together, it wouldn't be like we'd planned. My life is a mess. I have no one, Luke. Absolutely no one. You would be my only friend, my only family.

For you to do that, for you to be that for me, after all of this . . . well, it wouldn't be fair to you. I'm paying for what my family did, and I want you to have better than this.

I'm so sorry.

I'll be watching the news for your release. I've been lying on the couch for three days now, just staring at the TV, watching the coverage, and crying a little. Okay, crying a whole lot.

And I'll cry when I see you leave prison. But they'll be happy tears, Luke. Because it was all worth it.

Love,
Audrey

Dear Audrey—

You're a ditz, you know that? (No offense.)

Joke, Audrey. Joke. I know there's not much to joke about right now, but you sound so down and I just want to make you smile a little bit.

Don't you know that you're not going to watch me on TV? You're going to *be* on TV. Right there next to me. How am I going to kiss you and hold you and smell you if you're in your living room watching me walk out of prison?

I get it though. If anyone gets what you're going through right now—the loneliness, the doubt, the hurt and the tears—it's me. So let me make this loud and clear. To quote something a very wise woman once told me: You, Audrey Rutledge, are worth more than what you've been forced to believe. (I told you I had all your letters memorized. Plus I have them all here in front of me, and that's exactly what you told me when I was in the same place that you are right now.) The only thing I had back then was you and God. That's what saw me through.

And you're going to get through this, Audrey, because you have me and you have God. Do you understand that? You have me. Not because I feel obligated, but because I love you and I want to spend the rest of my life with you. And because I think you're really, really hot.

I hope that made you smile. But I didn't say it just to make you smile. I said it because I think you're hot. And beautiful. Inside and out. You are perfect and you are wonderful and I'm going to spend the rest of my life making sure you know that.

My dad actually did come see me—and he brought my little sister! She's not so little anymore. Wow. I just couldn't believe how much she's grown up in two years. I could tell that he felt really bad about not believing that I was innocent. It was almost painful to watch him stumble along as he tried to apologize, so I just stopped him and told him that it was alright. That I understood and that I loved him. It was amazing to see the look on his face. Forgiveness is a wonderful thing.

You and I are going to work on that together—forgiving your mom. Together. Because I'm here for you, Audrey, and I love you. Have I made that clear yet? Do I need to say it a million more times? I'll be glad to. I'll say it as much as I need to until you believe me.

My lawyer's working on stuff. He said something about getting a pardon from the governor and I said I didn't want a pardon, I wanted to be exonerated. But he said getting a pardon would be the quickest thing and then we could work on a new trial or getting the old conviction overturned or whatever. I said that sounded good. He told me again that he doesn't think it will be very long because of all the publicity. Thank goodness we live in football country.

He'll be calling you to let you know exactly when I'm getting out and I'm counting on you being here. Don't let me down, Audrey. And please make sure you smell good.

All my love,
Luke

PENNINGTON FREED

LEWISTON—Luke Pennington was released from prison today after Ellen Rutledge confessed to the murders and rapes of 19-year-old Heather Goodlet and 20-year-old Stacy Kemp. Pennington has been on death row for over a year following his wrongful conviction of the death of his girlfriend and her roommate nearly three years ago.

Pennington was accompanied by his family and his girlfriend, Audrey Rutledge, who is the daughter of Ellen Rutledge and the sister of former NFL rookie Trevor Rutledge. Both Pennington and Rutledge declined comment when asked about their relationship, but according to Pennington's attorney, Curtis Weaver, the two met after Pennington sought Rutledge out, asking her help to find evidence to clear his name. Weaver told reporters that Rutledge's belief in Pennington's innocence and her subsequent independent investigation into the facts of the case ultimately led to the arrest of her own mother.

Ellen Rutledge confessed to murdering the girls in order to cover up the hit-and-run death of Tracie Ann Watson by her son, Trevor Rutledge, nearly five years ago. NFL fans were shocked earlier this month when Rutledge turned himself in to authorities and confessed to hitting and killing Watson after an evening of drinking and driving. Rutledge was a top pick in last year's NFL draft and passed for 3,421 yards with 22 touchdowns.

Dear Audrey—

My therapist thinks I should write you letters. I was telling him about how we used to write to each other when I was in Polunsky and he said it might be therapeutic if I did it again. I'm not sure if he wants me to actually give them to you or not, but I probably will. I kind of miss writing to you, and I definitely miss getting letters from you. Those were the only happy times I had while I was in there—reading your letters. Whenever one came in, I was always so excited (even though half the time you were telling me something that drove me crazy, one way or another). So, anyway, I decided to take his advice and start writing to you every now and then. Delivery is going to be a lot different than it was before though.

Speaking of therapists, I really wish you would think about what I said about switching. I know you want to go to a Christian therapist, and that's fine, but just because someone's a Christian doesn't mean they're good at what they do, and I'm pretty sure yours is not. Do you really think you're getting any better? I don't see it. Don't get me wrong, you can cry on my shoulder every day for the rest of our lives and you can stay in your apartment and never go out again if you want. That's not what this is about. This is about the fact that you don't have any joy anymore, Audrey. I just want you to be happy.

Please don't think that I don't understand, because I do. I know you're going through a lot . . . I know. And I know it's going to take time. Maybe a lot of time. That's okay. I've got all the time in the world. Just don't give up on me, okay, Audrey?

But anyway, I want to tell you something. I guess one of the reasons I was kind of anxious to write to you again was because sometimes it's easier for me to tell you something in a letter than it is in person. I like it better when I can think about what I want to say and make sure it's worded right. And I've been thinking a lot about how to say this.

This isn't a big deal, it really isn't, but I've been kind of hesitant to tell you about it because I'm not really sure how you're going to react. I don't want to keep anything from you though. I don't want to keep any secrets from you. So, here it is.

I went to Heather's grave last week. Please don't read too much into this. This doesn't have anything to do with you or how much I love you. I hope you understand that. I hope you know that you are everything to me and that I love you so much. You are beautiful and wonderful and perfect and I want to spend the rest of my life convincing you of that. But when Heather died, I didn't even get to go to her funeral. I never got to say goodbye. I just wanted to talk to her about some things. It's just something that I needed to do.

I've got to go or I'm going to be late meeting you. One thing about prison was at least I always had plenty of time to write. Things are a lot busier on the outside. I love it though, and I love you.

All my love,
Luke

Dear Luke,

It is easier to say some things in a letter than it is to say them out loud, isn't it? Maybe it shouldn't be that way, though. Maybe this points to some huge deficit in our relationship, because this is not the way I pictured things going.

Me. You. Unable to be completely honest about what's going on.

So I think I'll write you a letter. You know that I'm doing it, of course. I'm looking at you right now, as you sit back on the couch with my feet in your lap, watching the dumbest show I've ever seen on TV (seriously, what is this crap that you're always watching?) and glancing over at me with a grin every few minutes.

And you've just leaned over and kissed me. Again. We certainly know how to do that with each other, but words?

Words are hard sometimes.

You look happy. I know you've got to be going through a lot. I know it's probably a mess inside your head, just like it is in mine. But you do a good job of hiding it, Luke. Your new shirts are already fitting a little loose after just a month of getting back to running. Your hair looks so much better with a little gel. And your face . . .

I can still see that bruise in the back of my mind. You never told me how you got it.

But you do things like that. Tuck little secrets away, put on a smile, and act like we're really okay, like we're a normal couple.

We're so NOT normal.

Why didn't you tell me that you were going to visit Heather's grave? I wouldn't have freaked out about it. Of course, I am freaking out about it now because you only told me afterward, like it was something that needed to be hidden from me. Why would you hide that? Sure, you've told me now, but clearly you thought there was a reason not to tell me when you took the road trip out of town last week to drive out there, "talk to her," and have your moment. You know she's not there, right? That saying whatever you said was about you, not her, right? And that sounds awful, and I'm a horrible person for saying it. But why did you keep me out of that part of your life? Is this just another compartment that I'm not allowed into?

It wasn't going to be like this. You were going to be released, and being together was going to come so naturally to us both, just like it seemed to in our letters. I knew you then. Really knew you. I loved you. I still love you, but I don't understand you. It wasn't going to be like this! It was going to be so easy, so good, so right . . .

And now, half of my family is in jail. I have a boyfriend who says he'll be here as long as it takes, but he's not even here, fully here, half the time.

And I'm writing horrible things about a dead girl because I'm a horrible, sick, twisted person. Just like my mother. Exactly like my mother.

What if I'm just like her, Luke?

If, God willing, I get past any of this to have a healthy relationship with someone that leads to marriage, that leads to children . . . how am I going to explain to my children what their grandmother did? What their own flesh and blood is capable of? How their own mother could be just as crazy and awful and manipulative and heartless . . .

I'm fighting back tears, Luke. Even now, as you rub my feet and laugh out loud at this ridiculous show that you watch all the freaking time. And you're not seeing me, even when you look over at me. Which is good, because if I was sobbing, like I do too often these days, you'd pull me into your arms. And I couldn't stand it but couldn't refuse.

Because I want you and I can't handle this all at the same time.

Maybe I do need a new therapist.

Or maybe you just need to find someone else.

I'm sorry, Luke. I don't know what to do.

Audrey

Audrey—

I am fully here. All the time. And I see you. All the time. I see a lot more than you think I do.

What I see, Audrey, is someone who is slipping away from me. Someone who needs more help than I can give her. Not because I don't want to, but because I don't know what to do.

Yes, it's a mess inside my head, and that's where I keep everything. How can I tell you anything bad that's in there when you can't even handle what's inside your own head? I don't tell you things because I don't want to make things worse for you. How much worse can they actually get before I lose you? You are so fragile, Audrey. I'm scared to death that one day I'm going to come over here and you're going to be gone.

I think we should be seeing some kind of progress by now. I think you should be getting better. But you're not. I know you're not, and you know it too.

I know I keep telling you to get a new therapist because the one you have right now obviously isn't doing you any good, but apparently what I'm doing for you isn't doing you any good either. Trying to stay positive . . . trying not to burden you with anything else. Maybe that's not what you need.

Maybe what you need is to know that you can talk to me about anything, and that I am willing to talk to you about anything. You want to know where that bruise on my cheek came from? New guard, that's all. He just wanted to see how I'd react. Wasn't a big deal. You learn real quick not to say anything on the phone or in letters because that just makes it worse. Things like that happened more than I care to admit. Not always to me, but to plenty of the guys I was with in there. They were real people, Audrey. Real people with real families and real feelings. And at night when I'm lying on my comfy pillow-top mattress in the quiet of my air-conditioned room, I remember them. I can hear them every time I close my eyes.

And then there's Heather and the guilt I feel for what happened to her and the guilt I feel for moving on with you and the guilt I feel for not even knowing what kind of relationship she had with God and whether or not she's with Him now.

You wanted me to be honest with you? Well, fine, because I'm tired of pretending that everything's okay whenever I'm around you. If I thought it would help you, I'd do it forever, but obviously it's not working.

So what do you need, Audrey? Do you need to hear about every dark thought that's in my head and every terrible thing that happened to me and every ounce of guilt that I'm feeling? Ask me anything you want and I'll give you every last detail. Do you need to turn into a shrieking harpy and yell and scream and take it all out on someone? I'm right here. I will do *anything* to help you get through this.

No, we're never going to be a normal couple . . . neither one of us are ever going to be normal. And our relationship may not ever be how either one of us pictured it when we were imagining our future. But that doesn't matter to me, Audrey. I love you and I want to be with you and I want to make this work. We just need to figure out how to do this. Together. Remember that? Remember *together*?

Remember how it felt when we prayed with each other? I have been praying for you every day, but I think we need to do that again . . . I think we need to pray—together. And I think we need to go see someone—together.

Please look up from this letter and nod. Please let me know that together is what you want, too.

Love,
Luke

Dear Luke,

Thank you.

Just . . . thank you.

I didn't realize that nodding at you, while I read that last letter, would prompt all of this. I can still picture you fighting back tears as you let out the breath you'd been holding. I thought you'd hug me, kiss me, move closer to me. I couldn't imagine why you jumped up from the couch, went into my room, and packed a bag for me. (And you packed all the wrong things, Luke. Which is why I had to borrow your toothbrush without asking. Sorry about that.)

It wasn't until we'd been in the car an hour, with you holding my hand in your lap as you drove, that I figured out where we were going. I thought at first that you were checking me into some facility. I was wondering how I was going to afford that, but before I could begin to add that to all the stress I've been feeling, we were out of the city, heading straight to a place I'd been before.

288

Your mom's house.

How did you know that the right thing to do for me was to sit around a table, eating dinner with you and your mom? How could you know how badly I needed those hours you and I spent out back sitting on the porch swing, talking through all that's been going on? How did you know that praying with me would make me begin to feel like maybe, just maybe, there's a light at the end of this tunnel I'm walking through?

You're so strong. In all the time I've known you, you've been so strong. Surviving that unfair sentence and those days in prison, adjusting to life again when everything changed, saying goodbye to Heather, facing the fallout of my mother's actions with me . . .

You're the strongest man I know, Luke.

And I trust you. So completely.

I'm so thankful that you reminded me of that passage in James, about how difficulties are something we're going to face, about how they produce endurance and greater faith. I know it in my head, but I'm beginning to work it out in my heart as we wait for what lies ahead. When we prayed over every part of our lives that is hurting right now, I knew you were working it out in your heart, too.

Being somewhere different, here with you, where it feels like reality can stay away for a while . . . it helps, Luke. Saying what I'm feeling, hearing you communicate the same . . . it's what I needed. And I'll do what you asked, as you held me close and told me that you're never going to give up on me.

I'll get help. We'll do this together.

Thank you for sharing your mom and letting me be part of your family tonight. Thank you for being a good sport as I watched those old home videos of you running in high school and laughed at your hair. Thank you for all the sweet kisses and the words you prayed over me when we said goodnight. Thank you for sleeping on the sofa so that I could stay in your room.

Thanks for helping me through this.

I love you. So, so much. And when I give you this letter tomorrow, I think it's going to be the beginning of a better season for us both.

Love,
Audrey

Dear Luke,

I haven't felt the need to write to you in a long time, but after today, I think it might do me some good. And like Dr. Bailey always tells us, healing is a process, and if we have to write each other letters for the rest of our lives . . . well, so be it. It's part of who we are, after all.

Can I start by saying how adorable you were today? Seriously, Luke. I could tell that you were nervous about meeting my dad. He's the one who should have been nervous about meeting you, after what you went through because of our family, but I could feel how sweaty your hands were as we waited for him at that awful restaurant he'd picked out. What did you think he'd do? Tell you that he didn't want his daughter, who he hadn't even cared enough to see in six months, dating an ex-con? (Like he can talk. Wow, Luke, look at me. Actually trying to see the humor in all of this. That's progress, right?)

But it worked out. I can tell he's trying to make peace with the whole situation. He didn't even lose his composure when I told him we were going to go visit Mom after we finished lunch.

I think you were probably more nervous about meeting her than you were about meeting him. (And I'm a great girlfriend for springing it all on you in the same day, huh?)

Nervous or not, I sure did need you there. You've been amazing during all the visits we've made to Trevor this fall, though I know it can't be easy to go back into that environment, even as a free man. I can see you flinch as doors are bolted shut, and I know it highlights painful memories that will never go away. I spend most of these visits praying for Trevor and praying for God to heal your heart even more, day by day, little by little.

I could see evidence of what He's already done when you met my mom. You were so full of grace and compassion, Luke. She didn't deserve it, despite apologizing for all that she'd done, despite struggling not to cry as we talked to her. Your impact statement about not wanting to see her receive the death sentence meant more to her than either one of us could have fathomed at the time, and I could see it in her eyes as she thanked you in person. You were so good to us both, showing her mercy as we talked, then holding me and letting me cry once we left.

I do that less and less these days, but sometimes . . . sometimes it helps.

Hey, you know what else helps? You. Yes, you, the hottest, most incredible man in all of Houston. (And quite possibly Texas. I don't know, though. It's a big state.) When we got in the car, I was pretty sure it was going to be a long, hard drive back. That is, until you started quizzing me for our final, at which point I knew, without a doubt, that it would be a long, hard drive back. I never should have agreed to take that poli sci class with you. You're so arrogant! You think you know more of the answers than I do. I've totally kicked your butt on every test this semester, Luke. And I plan on kicking your butt on every exam in law school once we get there. And then winning more cases than you do after we pass the bar exam: Rutledge and Pennington, Attorneys at Law.

No shame in losing to a girl, Luke.

You'll do well to remember that on our long run tomorrow afternoon. I know I'm supposed to take it slow at this point in the training (like you keep lecturing me every time we hit the pavement), but since this is my second marathon and your first, I feel like my experience allows me to make the call to pick up the pace. (Who am I kidding, right? I know you're intentionally being conservative with your pace, just so you won't leave me behind. Thanks, seriously. It's so amazing that you turned out to be exactly the kind of guy I told you I liked, those who opened doors and bought flowers, plus the kind who won't let me run alone, even if I'm a lot slower than you are. I love that about you, you know.)

See? I started this letter because I was feeling down about my mom, but I'm smiling like an idiot now. Writing to you has helped. I knew it would when we prayed together before you left tonight, as you're likely praying for me even now. And that kiss you gave me, right before you said goodnight, made me want to pull you back into my apartment and kiss you some more. It's so hard to say goodnight these days.

But I need to say goodnight now. It's an early morning at church tomorrow. We're scheduled to work the nursery during the contemporary service, so we'll both need every second of sleep we can get. (And have I mentioned how adorable you are? Especially as you're attempting a conversation with a one-year-old who can only laugh at you, I think because your hair sticks up kind of funny in the back. And as you're entertaining the preschoolers with puppets, trying to tell them a Bible story and sing songs. I love watching you with them. You're going to be a great daddy someday.)

I'm glad this hard day is done . . . and I'm glad you were there with me.

I'll never stop thanking God for bringing you to me, no matter how unconventional the path was. You are so, so loved, Luke Pennington.

Love,
Audrey

Dear Audrey—

One night, what seems like a long time ago, I asked you to look up at me and nod . . . to let me know that you were willing to do whatever it took to get better. Whatever it took so that we could be together . . . really together.

And you have come so far since then—we both have. Look at what we did yesterday. We can get through anything now, I just know it. And I just know that you are going to be all right. I'll admit that my heart stopped for a fraction of a second when you handed me that letter, but then I realized it made sense that you'd have some stuff to work through. Actually, it would have made less sense if you didn't. And when we're going through something, that's what we're supposed to do, right? Talk about it or write about it, and there's no shame in that. Yes, you have made a lot of progress and you amaze me every day. You are the strongest, bravest, smartest, most beautiful woman in the world, and I don't know what I'd do without you. I don't ever want to find out. I want to spend the rest of my life with you. I've told you that before, but now I'm telling you in a different way . . . a way that I know we're both ready for.

I'll never stop thanking God for bringing you to me, either. And you are so, so loved, too, Audrey Rutledge.

Speaking of which, though, I don't want to work with you at Rutledge and Pennington, or even Pennington and Rutledge. (Seriously, Audrey, did you really think your name was going to go first?)

I would, however, be honored to work with you at Pennington and Pennington, and if you would look up at me and nod again now, it would make me the happiest man in the world.

What do you say, Audrey? Will you marry me?

All my love,
Luke

Dear Luke,

Wow. You never told me that you snore!

And I'm not talking a cute little breathy sound. I'm talking a loud, deep, scary sound that is so powerful the walls around us just might fall down. Seriously, I'm sitting here in bed, watching you as the sun begins to rise, completely shocked that this is my new reality for the next fifty, sixty, seventy years. It's my first morning to wake up as Audrey Pennington, and I'm thinking that I should have checked the fine print on your sleeping habits before I said "I do."

I still would have said it, though. Even though you're snoring loud enough to wake up all of humanity.

It's a good thing you whisked me away to such a remote place last night, given the noise you're making. I'll admit that I was nervous when you wouldn't tell me where we were going, but that probably goes without saying. I was nervous all day. Not just about last night, either, but also about all the details of the wedding. I'm not sure how the planning goes for girls who have mothers who can help them and family members there to pick up the slack on the big day, but it was hectic for me, wasn't it? And for you, too, since you stepped up and did more than your fair share to make sure the day was perfect.

Which it was. Sure, my dad showed up to the church late (it was a hard day for him, without my mom here), your little sister brought a boyfriend no one even knew about (your dad looked like he was about to have a coronary), your brother's wife kept having contractions before the ceremony (what is she, forty-three weeks pregnant?), and your mother cried like you were going back to prison (because marriage is like a ball and chain, she said). It was nutty, Luke. All of it.

But it was perfect. Why? Because you were standing there at the front, waiting for me, looking at me like no one else was even in the church.

And your vows! You never told me you were going to write your own vows. You never told me that you were going to write them as another letter. You never told me that you'd say out loud, there in the presence of God as we made our marriage covenant together, all the words you'd wanted to whisper in my ear when there was bulletproof glass between us and not enough time to say everything we felt.

It was perfect. The most perfect day after the most difficult year of my life, something that God worked through because He brought me closer to Him and He brought you to me.

I get emotional even thinking about it. I got emotional then, too, of course. Oh, the tears. So many tears I cried as you said those sweet words. It wasn't pretty crying either, but you looked at me like I was beautiful. I *feel* beautiful.

Especially now, now that you're waking up and have finally stopped snoring. Especially now, with your hand on my thigh, your chest pressed against my shoulder, your lips on my neck, and your smile . . . I can feel you smiling against my skin. Probably because I'm blushing, because the experience of waking up next to you is very new, and because I'm grinning now, knowing exactly what you're thinking.

You're not going to let me finish this letter. Whatever. I'm good with that.

Because all the words we still have left to say . . .

. . . well, we have the rest of our lives to say them.

Love,
Audrey

Dear Audrey—

Wow. How long has it been since I've written you a letter? At least a year I think . . . I really can't even remember the last time. But don't be alarmed. Yes, I woke up and couldn't go back to sleep, but it wasn't a panic attack and you were sound asleep, so I just got up. Don't worry. I've got a lot on my mind, but no panic . . . at least not much.

I had some ice cream, watched some TV, and then decided that maybe writing to you would be a good way to sort out everything that's in my head. Like the good old days.

By the way, I know you're going to be mad, but I changed the alarm. You need your sleep and I think we should just do five miles today anyway. I really want to put our marathon on hold right now. I know what you said, but I still can't believe all that running could possibly be a good idea. We'll talk to the doctor on Thursday, though, and I promise to go along with whatever she says.

The doctor. On Thursday. I can't believe it. Do you really think they're going to be able to hear a heartbeat already?

After I woke up, I looked at you lying there next to me for a long time. You told me once that you weren't a pretty sleeper, but that's not true. You're beautiful. Even more now that I know you're carrying our child. Everything seems the same but so completely different. I mean . . . all of a sudden there is this whole other person in our lives! I know you thought I wasn't happy when you told me, but that's not true. I was just kind of in shock. This is the biggest thing that has ever happened to us (and considering what we've been through, that's saying a lot!), plus this wasn't exactly what we had planned. But God has better plans for us than we have for ourselves.

Am I worried? A bit, yes. I think that's normal. Normal for anyone, right? How could I suddenly find out I'm going to be a dad without being at least a little bit worried? I know you're worried, too, but Audrey—I *promise* you that you are going to be the best mother in the world. This baby is already so blessed to have you as its mother. You haven't even known about this baby for twenty-four hours and you've already put your foot down and said that there was no way we were naming it Squid. See? Such a great mom.

I love you, Audrey. And I love our baby. This is going to be the most awesome thing we've ever done.

And I guess I'd better stop writing because there goes the alarm . . .

Time to run.

All my love,

Luke

~The End~

Thank you for taking the time to read *Run*—we hope you have enjoyed it as much as we enjoyed writing it! Be sure to visit us on Amazon to find more Christian fiction that we wrote together such as our second book—*Obsessed*—or some of our individual novels. Please consider connecting with us on one of the following sites (because we would love to hear from you)! It is a privilege to try to help others deepen their walk with Christ through sharing our characters with readers, and we are thankful for each one of you.

www.LNCronk.com
http://www.jennfaulk.com
www.LNCronk.blogspot.com
https://www.facebook.com/jennfaulkbooks
www.Facebook.ReadChopChop.com

www.ingramcontent.com/pod-product-compliance
Lightning Source LLC
Chambersburg PA
CBHW071251170626
46809CB00001B/170